"We have to put l
after a few moments ha
and resolute. "That's the only way this will work."

"Is that really what you want?"

Carrie folded her arms across her chest. What she wanted was for him to take her downstairs to her suite and pick up where they were interrupted in the elevator the night before. No, wait. What she wanted to do was travel back in time and erase what had happened between them altogether.

But that didn't feel right either.

Carrie sighed. She couldn't change the past. She couldn't change the fact they had shared one of the most intense, passionate moments of her life. That Jack had touched her in places she still blushed to think about. They had been prepared to die together, and in that state of mind, let go of all inhibitions and thrown common sense to the wind.

"That's how it has to be." She forced herself to meet his probing gaze. "Last night was a mistake, Jack, plain and simple. We are just going to have to move on."

He leaned in far closer than necessary. Electricity tingled between them. "You can think last night was a mistake if you want to, but this isn't over," he informed her, his breath hot on her skin. "Not by a long shot."

Tempting Fate

by

Gwen Kleist

Tempting Fate

Cover Art by *Diana Carlile*

The Wild Rose Press, Inc.
PO Box 708
Adams Basin, NY 14410-0708
Visit us at www.thewildrosepress.com

Publishing History
First Edition, 2021
Trade Paperback ISBN 978-1-5092-3805-7
Digital ISBN 978-1-5092-3806-4

Published in the United States of America

Dedication

In loving memory of my mom, Suzanne,
who always encouraged, supported, and believed in me,
though I don't know if a steamy romance novel
was what she had in mind

Chapter One

Had it been anyone else but herself in this predicament, Carolyn Thomas would have laughed.

But it wasn't anyone else. She was the one stuck in a revolving glass door, her leather tote wedged sideways between the curved wall and the door's rubber edge.

The part that made her want to laugh? Trapped right beside her was the jerk who caused the jam. On second thought, maybe cry was a better word. She couldn't believe her terrible luck.

"Pull harder," he ordered, taking the liberty of grabbing one of the pink leather handles. The brand-new bag was the trendiest color of the season and cost more money than Carrie could honestly afford.

"That's a Coach bag." She swatted his hand away. "Don't touch it."

The man raised his palms in mock surrender and stepped back.

His sarcasm fueled her annoyance, and Carrie glared in his direction.

He met her angry gaze, and damn if he wasn't one of the hottest men she had ever seen. The clear-cut lines of his profile loomed above her, his tan face deepened against the starched white collar of his shirt. Dark eyes pierced her, accusing, as if it were her fault he couldn't wait one second for the next opening in the revolving

1

door. Instead, he had rushed in behind her with such force, the door jerked forward, catching her bag and nearly yanking her arm off with it.

"I've got somewhere I need to be," he said, making no further effort to help.

Carrie pressed her lips together, stifling the tart reply threatening to escape. She returned her attention to freeing the bag, tugging and twisting, but it would not break loose.

Caught between the air-conditioned lobby of the Grand Portofino Resort & Casino and the brutal heat of the Las Vegas summer sun, their little glass triangle grew hotter by the second. At last, she sighed and let go of the bag, sliding a hand across her beaded brow. Her wavy blonde hair stuck to her neck, and she lifted it off her skin in an effort to cool off.

The man assessed her with insolent curiosity, then his expression softened. "Let's try pushing the door back the other way."

Drawing a deep breath, Carrie met his gaze. Why should she acknowledge his offer to help with any kind of gratitude? The guy acted like he was doing her a favor, when this ridiculous situation was his fault.

He loosened his tie and unbuttoned his collar. "Hold on to your bag, and I'll push."

Carrie obeyed wordlessly, gripping the pink straps as he pushed the door. It didn't budge.

His broad shoulders and bicep muscles flexed underneath his suit jacket, stretching the tailored charcoal-gray material as they worked to free the jam. Had he been a stranger passing by, she would have found herself staring shamelessly at his chiseled good looks. But right now, his arrogance doused all the qualities she might have otherwise found attractive.

He gave up with a grunt, raking the light brown hair that had fallen across his forehead back into place. "Haven't you ever heard of a nice little purse?"

"Haven't you ever heard it's rude to jump into a revolving door with another person?"

"I was in a rush."

"And that's my problem?" She stared him down, biting her tongue to keep the words she wanted to say from tumbling out. Right now, she should be inside the hotel presenting her pitch to Robert Dillon, owner of the Grand Portofino. Instead, she was trapped in a *door*, of all places, with this guy.

She could almost see her boss's expression when she got back to New York and told Phyllis Dailey why she had blown the pitch.

Only a week ago, Phyllis had called Carrie into her office to brief her on the Grand Portofino. Robert Dillon had bought the bankrupt Desert Star Hotel two years ago and had since spent millions rebuilding the one-time gem of the Vegas Strip. The Grand Portofino had opened less than a month ago and promised to be one of the most exclusive casino resorts in the city. Mr. Dillon was looking for a new agency to take over its PR.

And Cresswell & Dailey Public Relations was one of the top contenders.

"This could be a huge step in your career," Phyllis had said. "Pull this off, and I just know you'll make partner. I'm putting a lot of faith in you, Carrie, so don't let me down."

Phyllis's words haunted Carrie now. Ten minutes late to what might possibly be the most important meeting of her career, she stood trapped within the confines of a narrow glass triangle, trying to free her bag without ruining everything inside it.

Boy, was Phyllis ever going to be disappointed. It would have been bad enough if Carrie bungled the presentation, but to not even make the meeting in time. She shuddered at the thought.

A bang on the glass door snapped her attention back to the problem at hand.

Outside, a valet had finally noticed the immobile revolving door. "Is everything all right, sir?"

"No, everything is not all right," her cellmate spat. "This woman's bag jammed the door. Get some help."

Carrie glared at him. The valet hurried through the other door next to them and into the hotel.

He ignored her icy stare. Instead of apologizing, he looked away and shifted in discomfort. The valet approached from the lobby side of the door, with two other young men wearing bellhop uniforms. When they reached the revolving door, the valet said, "We're going to push it toward the street."

The man nodded and faced the street, hands against the glass. To Carrie, he mumbled gruffly, "Hold on to your bag."

"It wouldn't hurt to show a little common courtesy." She bristled at his order but clutched the pink leather handle of her Coach tote as he instructed.

No response. Carrie glowered at him with disbelief.

"After all," she pointed out. "This whole thing is your fault, not mine."

Silence.

He had a lot of nerve ignoring her.

The valet asked, "Ready, sir?"

"Let's do it."

Irritated by his disregard, Carrie let go of the strap and jabbed his arm with her forefinger. "I can't believe you have the audacity to ignore me when—"

With four men pushing the revolving glass door, at last it jerked into motion. The door hit her in the rear and sent her flying to the sidewalk in front of the hotel's entrance. She landed on her hands and knees as a very unladylike grunt fell from her lips.

Laughter rumbled over her as Carrie rose, pushing her hair off her face. She smoothed her gray skirt suit and eased her foot back into its red-soled stiletto, nearly falling again as she struggled to regain her balance. Pain shot through her leg. She looked down and saw a gaping run in her pantyhose, and blood bubbled up on her skinned knee.

The valet was instantly at her side. "Are you all right, miss?"

Ignoring him, she met the man with a gaze as fiery as her demand. "I suppose you find this funny?"

"Honey, this is the best laugh I've had in weeks."

"Don't call me honey!" Carrie shot, defiance fresh on her tongue. She grabbed her bag from the bellhop, who had retrieved it from the ground, with a bit more hostility than intended, then spun around. She winced again as pain shot through her twisted ankle. Doing her best to ignore it, she limped through the hotel door with exaggerated dignity. The sound of his laughter mocked her as she entered the hotel, fueling her retreat.

The lobby of the Grand Portofino Resort & Casino transported her to the Italian Riviera. She paused for a moment to get her bearings, taking in the space as she scanned it for the hotel's check-in counter. The floors were sleek marble, and graceful pillars, waterfalls, and abundant plant life adorned the space. Even the furniture was reminiscent of the Riviera, with splashes of bright color and stylish beachy decor. Sunlight flooded the expansive room through skylights in the soaring ceiling. Off to the side, a tuxedoed gentleman played a baby grand piano, filling the Grand Portofino's lobby with the sophisticated swell of classical music.

But the elegant surroundings did little to mellow Carrie's mood. Her ankle throbbing, she spotted what she was looking for and hobbled across the lobby.

"I have a five o'clock appointment with Robert Dillon." She handed her business card to a clerk behind the registration desk. "I'm afraid I'm a bit late."

With a pleasant smile, the clerk lifted the telephone and dialed an extension. "Carolyn Thomas is here for Mr. Dillon. I see. Yes, I'll tell her. Thank you."

She placed the receiver down and smiled again. "They haven't started yet, Ms. Thomas. The meeting is in the conference room on the thirtieth floor. You can go right up."

For the first time since arriving in Las Vegas, the knot in her chest began to untangle. She smiled gratefully as the clerk pointed her toward the east elevator bank.

"Do you have any luggage?" the clerk inquired.

"I left it with the valet."

"I'll make sure it's brought to your room. Mr. Dillon has arranged for you to stay in one of our suites."

Before heading to the elevator, she popped into the ladies' room to fix her hair and makeup. She studied herself in the mirror of the hotel's plush lounge, knowing she needed to pull it together, but still pissed at the man who had left her so unraveled.

"Shake it off," Carrie instructed her reflection in a stern hushed voice, dabbing on the pink-tinted lip gloss that always gave her a fresh dose of confidence.

She examined her leg and frowned. The pain in her ankle had subsided, but it was swollen just the same. That she could deal with; it was her knee she was worried about. Skinned raw by the cement, she looked like a tomboy. There was a gaping run in her hose that stretched from her knee all the way up her thigh. There was no way she could pitch a multimillion-dollar account looking like this.

With no time to locate her luggage for a fresh pair of pantyhose, she peeled off her torn ones and hoped Mr. Dillon wouldn't mind bare legs. Then she dabbed the cut on her knee with a damp paper towel to wipe away the blood, washed her hands, and exited the ladies' room.

Carrie took a deep breath as she walked toward the elevators, relieved to finally be on her way upstairs to give her presentation. She loved this part of her job.

She pressed the Up button and waited, her gaze darting between the six elevators and their small digital monitors announcing where it was currently positioned. She checked the time on her phone for the tenth time since landing in Las Vegas and shook her head in disbelief at this miserable day.

David had called at six thirty this morning to remind her to leave a key so he could pick up the last of his stuff while she was gone. Talking to her ex-fiancé always put her in a cranky mood. Then the taxi driver dropped her at the wrong terminal, and she ran across

Kennedy International Airport only to find her flight delayed by an hour. The revolving glass door incident threw yet another wrench into her carefully planned schedule.

And now, these elevators refused to work. "Come on," she muttered, as she pressed the button again. Nothing.

What else could go wrong today?

She was just about to lose her cool when all six elevators suddenly kicked into motion. She hurried into the first one to arrive and pressed the button for the thirtieth floor.

"Hold the elevator." A voice boomed through the elevator bank, echoing along with the heavy slap of men's shoes racing across the Grand Portofino's marble floor. Carrie sighed and held open the door.

And in stepped the man from the revolving glass door.

Her breath caught in her lungs at the unexpected sight. He also did a double take but then astonished her with a smile and friendly, "Hello again."

"Hi," Carrie returned, guarded, and more than a little annoyed. Six elevators all going up, and he had to step onto hers.

Standing in the corner and pretending to look at her phone as the elevator ascended, she tried not to notice the man's gaze tracing her long legs and slender hips. But when she felt them settle on her face, she turned to him with uninhibited self-assurance. She met his gaze straight on and raised her eyebrows, questioning his brazen gesture.

"Lose your hose?" he asked, raising an eyebrow. His smile was infectious.

Despite herself, Carrie chuckled, and he began laughing, as well. The sound of his laughter mirrored his voice, rich and deep. Her mood instantly lifted at the sound.

Her giggles subsided into a wide smile. "You owe me an apology." But the lightness of her voice revealed she had already accepted it. "And a new bag."

She lifted her Coach tote so he could inspect the damage. The pink leather was scuffed where the rubber edge of the revolving glass door had clamped it, causing it to look oddly misshapen and quite dirty.

"I'm claustrophobic," the man explained. "I guess getting stuck in that stupid door made me a little edgy. I'll buy you a new bag."

"Don't worry about it." Carrie let her arm drop to her side. "But there's still no excuse for laughing when I fell."

"Yeah, I'm really sorry," he offered, looking appropriately humbled. "Relief. I was just glad to be out of there." He glanced at her leg again. "How's your ankle?"

"It's fine." She lifted her foot in its high-heeled pump and examined it. "I think I just twisted it a little."

"Glad to hear it."

A smile still clinging to her face, Carrie examined him in a new light. His profile was the classic kind of handsome, warmer now that it had relaxed. Strong and confident, he radiated a sense of unspoken power. Laugh lines teased the corners of his eyes and mouth, but his dark brown eyes were bright and youthful. She imagined him to be around forty.

"I'm Carolyn Thomas, by the way."

A flash of recognition danced across his features,

and she wondered if perhaps he recognized her name from the PR world. But then he smiled again and said, "Nice to meet you, Ms. Thomas." Carrie was sure she must have misread his expression.

"Please, call me Carrie."

"Jack."

She took his outstretched hand and shook it, but the pleasantries came to a screeching halt when the elevator lurched to a stop and the lights flashed off. With her hand still clasped in his, she fell against his hard chest, and they both tumbled to the floor.

She clutched his arm, barely able to make him out in the hazy yellow emergency light. "What's happening?" Her voice trembled in the hushed stillness.

"I think the elevator stopped." Jack peeled her fingers off the sleeve of his suit jacket and pushed his body to a standing position. "Are you okay?"

Carrie nodded but remained sitting on the floor. She grabbed her phone and searched for a signal. Jack pressed three buttons on the elevator panel at random, then pounded it several times with the brunt of his fist and shouted a swear word.

She rose to her feet, remembering. "Oh God…you're claustrophobic."

Jack clasped his hands behind his head and turned away. "Yes, I know that," he sneered.

She placed a hand on his shoulder, but he ducked away. "Lady, you are bad luck."

"Hey." Carrie's voice rose. "This is *not* my fault."

Jack turned to face her, his eyes bright with panic, and the color drained from his face. He took a deep breath and swallowed. "Okay, let's remain calm."

"Yes. Calm," she repeated. But this was no

revolving glass door they were trapped inside. This was an elevator. A big metal box suspended—she glanced at the floor numbers—nineteen stories in the air. Nineteen stories! Her stomach tightened. "Is there a phone in here?"

"I just tried, and it's not working." Jack shook his head. "And my damn cell phone is dead."

"Mine's not getting a signal, anyway," she said. But she was determined to stay optimistic. "Let's holler for help."

"Nobody would hear us. These elevators were built to be soundproof."

"Hmph." Carrie slid to the floor and hugged her legs to her chest, resting her chin against the roughness of her skinned knee.

Jack began pacing, but in the cramped space, it was more like walking in tight little circles. "It's hot in here," he murmured, fumbling with his tie knot again. Carrie realized the air conditioner was no longer working. The air grew thick and warm, and the faint scent of sweat began to permeate the space. She gave her armpit an inconspicuous sniff and thanked the BO gods that the smell wasn't coming from her.

She studied Jack in the dimness. Under the circumstances, she should be coming apart at the seams, but keeping this claustrophobic man at ease motivated her to stay composed. Evoking the words of her Saturday morning yoga class instructor, she forced herself to take a couple of deep, calming breaths. She did her best to keep them as discreet as possible, hoping he wouldn't notice. She thought about her meeting on the thirtieth floor. There was no chance of making it now.

A glimmer of hope edged its way into her mind. Maybe when she didn't show up, Robert Dillon would realize she must be stuck in one of the elevators. After all, the front desk clerk had called and told him she was on her way up. She smiled to herself. Help was probably already on the way.

Better not share her thoughts with Jack. No use in giving him false hope, just in case.

"Take off your jacket and have a seat," she advised, patting the floor beside her. "It looks like we're going to be here for a while."

Chapter Two

"So then what happened?"

Carrie closed her eyes, remembering the day she broke off her engagement. "I said, 'David, I love you, but we don't want the same things out of life.' And I left."

"Just like that?" Jack sat beside her, leaning against the wall of the elevator, his legs outstretched before him, ankles crossed. He fanned himself with a manila file folder which Carrie had pulled from her bag, clearly enjoying the cool breeze it created.

"Just like that." She pushed a damp tendril of hair off her forehead. She had already taken off her blazer. Jack had removed his suit jacket as well, along with his tie, and his crisp white shirtsleeves were rolled to his elbows. He offered the file folder to Carrie in a wordless gesture, but she shook her head and offered him a soft smile of appreciation.

"The thing is, I did love him, and I know he loved me, but I hated the person I became when I was with him."

Jack turned his head toward her. "How so?"

"Dave always thought I needed rescuing. He didn't trust me to think for myself. He meant well, and I know he would have been good to me. But he didn't respect me enough to realize I could think for myself and make my own decisions. I hated feeling so submissive." She

13

shook her head, lost in the memory. "I was starting to resent him."

Jack raised his eyebrows, and she gave him a guilty shrug. "I'm far too selfish to sacrifice my ideals to please a man."

"I don't think there's anything selfish about that."

She smiled, grateful for his validation. God knows she had spent enough time defending her decision to other people. Her father, for one, who thought she was crazy for not wanting to marry the successful sports agent. Of course, she couldn't help but wonder if Paul Thomas's grief sprang from her broken engagement, or from having to say goodbye to Yankees season tickets. David had charmed her parents from day one. Carrie often mused that when she ended things with her fiancé, her parents were more upset about losing David than he had been about losing her.

Their breakup had occurred almost four months ago, and although he had called her a couple of times, Carrie had managed to place all thoughts of her ex-fiancé out of her mind. She immersed herself in work, finding comfort and a new source of strength in her achievements at Cresswell & Dailey. Her career gave her confidence. It made her feel powerful, intelligent, and indispensable. She didn't care what her parents, or David or anyone else, for that matter, thought. Climbing the corporate ladder on her own was proving far more fulfilling than being married to a successful businessman.

Especially one who thought her greatest talent was her ability to iron his shirts.

Her sister Jill had married straight out of college, and by the time she was thirty, had two kids and a perfect house in Connecticut. Her parents were so proud, you'd think she had won a Nobel Prize, not married a stockbroker and given birth to twin boys.

Carrie often wondered if the reason she strived so hard to achieve her own goals was because she'd been trying to keep up with her older sister since they were little girls. She wasn't about to marry a rich man just to please her parents, but maybe becoming a success on her own would liberate her from a lifetime of existing in Jill's perfect shadow.

She sighed and leaned back against the wall of the elevator. She did want a husband and a family of her own someday. But one thing was certain. If she ever did fall in love and get engaged again, it wouldn't be to a man like David.

The whole situation now coaxed an ironic laugh out of her. Carrie turned to Jack in the sweltering elevator.

"Funny, the way we take life for granted. A few hours ago, I thought dealing with my broken engagement was my biggest problem." She glanced around the dark elevator. "That all seems so superficial now."

"We all take life for granted, Carrie. It's part of being human." He offered her his makeshift fan again, and this time she accepted it. "Things like this remind us to keep life in perspective."

Her eyes drifted shut as she fanned herself with the folder. Her white blouse was damp with sweat and clung to her breasts. She knew if he looked, Jack would be able to see the intricate lace pattern of her bra, and probably her nipples, too. She didn't care.

"It's eight thirty," he said, his voice low and grim.

Carrie opened her eyes. Jack was checking his watch. A gold Rolex.

She thumped her head twice against the wall. "Good Lord, I never knew time could drip by at such a snail's pace."

The warmth in Jack's voice seeped into her very core as he said, "At least we have each other to keep company."

"Yes." She placed a grateful hand on his arm. She didn't know what she would have done if she had to withstand this torture alone. Jack might have been the epitome of rudeness when they got stuck together in the revolving glass door, but his presence here in the elevator was proving nothing but a comfort.

"So how about you?" Carrie asked.

His gaze shot up. "How about me, what?"

She smiled coyly. "Is there someone at home wondering why you haven't made it home for dinner yet?"

"No." A hint of a chuckle rumbled through the word. "Just a bunch of stuffy men who have probably gotten tired of waiting for me and gone home themselves."

"So you're here on business." Carrie's deduction was an invitation for him to elaborate, but as she spoke, something above them caught her eye, and the question disappeared from her mind.

"Hey, do you think we could crawl through there?" She pointed her chin and gestured toward the ceiling.

Jack followed her gaze to the hatch door above them. "We could, but it wouldn't get us very far."

Determined to take action, Carrie bounced to her feet. She was accustomed to being in control. She handled PR campaigns and marketing budgets. She even took charge of her own love life. She was not about to let some man she just met tell her she had no control over something as instinctual as finding a way to save her own life. "It's worth a try."

"Now wait just a minute," Jack said, standing, as well. "You can't go crawling onto the roof of an elevator suspended twenty stories in the air."

"Nineteen."

"Nineteen, twenty…it doesn't matter. It's too dangerous."

A puff of air escaped Carrie's lips. "Dangerous? And you call sitting here doing nothing safe?"

Jack held her gaze as she wordlessly dared him to defy her. Waiting for help to arrive was proving fruitless, and they both knew it. It was time to take matters into their own hands.

"Okay." He stretched his arms forward and cracked his knuckles. "But I'm going up."

"Suit yourself, macho man." She laced her fingers together and offered him a boost.

Jack surveyed her delicate hands, then his own one-hundred-and-eighty-pound frame and laughed. "I'll crush you."

"I'm very strong," Carrie insisted, bracing her body to give Jack a lift. "Give me a little credit."

"The only thing I'm going to give you is a broken back," Jack said, ignoring her offer. Carrie let her hands drop as he valiantly jumped and pounded his fist against the door. On his third try, the door came loose and slid to the side of the roof. The blackness of the elevator shaft greeted them as they both looked up into the abyss.

She sighed. "Now what?"

Without warning, he swooped down and grabbed Carrie around her thighs. Over her shrieking protests, he instructed, "When I lift you, look and see if there are any doors open on the floors above us."

Carrie did as she was told, resenting Jack's stout order but at the same time enticed by his take-charge attitude. She allowed him to lift her through the hatch.

The elevator shaft stretched above her like a black, starless sky. A thin slit of light filtered in from high above, but the vast darkness squelched it before it could reach them. The deserted shaft offered no sign of help. She squinted and searched harder.

"What do you see?" Jack's voice was muffled against her skirt. His hot breath tickled her thighs.

"Nothing," she said, dejected. She kicked her feet lightly. "Let me down."

Jack loosened his grip. She sucked in her breath, exhilarated by the electric closeness as she slid down against his hard body. His gruff, stubbled chin scraped her skin as her arms fell around his neck. When Carrie's feet touched the ground, they were still pressed together, faces mere inches apart, eyes locked.

She blinked and then released his gaze and took a step back. Her heart fluttered from more than the thrill of being lifted through the ceiling of the elevator.

"Sorry." A muscle twitched on his jawline, and he turned away.

Carrie twisted her fingers together and paced the elevator. After a moment, Jack again jumped toward the ceiling, trying to grab hold of the open rim.

"Leave the door off," she requested. "Maybe we'll get some air circulating."

"I'm not trying to close it." His words bounced with the pace of his body. The elevator shook a little bit each time he hit the floor, and she placed her hand against the wall for support. Her stomach fluttered.

On his fourth try, Jack managed to grab hold of the rim, muscles flexing, dangling in the air for only a moment to catch his breath before hoisting himself onto the roof of the elevator.

"What are you doing?" Her voice was shaky. Standing alone in the elevator was wholly unnerving.

"Nothing." Jack's voice faded as he disappeared from her view.

She peered through the hatch, her throat tightening. "Hey," she called, shivering when she heard the echo of her own voice in response. Jack's face reappeared, a mere shadow looming against the blackness of the elevator shaft. Carrie asked again, "What are you doing up there?"

"I have to pee," Jack said, his words crisp and even. His face disappeared again.

"But where..." Carrie faltered back a step. "Oh."

She bit her lip, tilting her head in curiosity. After a few moments, Jack reappeared. He reached his arm through the hatch, offering to help her up. "Don't you have to go?"

She shook her head, not bothering to hide the wrinkles of disgust she was sure were plastered across her face. Jack lowered his tall frame through the hatch and jumped into the elevator, landing on all fours. The elevator shook with the force, and she gasped, placing her hand on the wall for balance. Then she slid down to sit on the floor beside him.

She placed a hand on Jack's wrist and tilted it to

read his watch. Damn, it was a nice Rolex. They were going on four hours.

Jack released a long, tired breath. "I think it's getting hotter in here."

"Take your shirt off," Carrie suggested.

"Take *your* shirt off."

Carrie wrinkled her nose at him. "You wish."

I do wish. Jack's playful expression said the words as clearly as if he'd spoken them. But he didn't say a thing. Instead, he took her advice and began unbuttoning his shirt.

She bit her lower lip, mesmerized by his commanding movements. She stared at his white cotton undershirt with envy and wished propriety didn't prevent her from sitting there in her underwear, too. He looked so cool and at ease. In her stifling blouse and sweat-drenched, pinching underwire bra, Carrie failed to even notice the muscular arms extending from his short sleeves.

Okay, that was a lie. She totally noticed. Even trapped in a hot, stalled elevator with bad lighting, only a blind woman wouldn't notice those guns. She wriggled in her own stifling clothes as she checked him out, unabashed.

Kicking off his shoes and socks, Jack exhaled. "So much better." He leaned back, closed his eyes, and Carrie thought he looked as relaxed as if lounging poolside in Palm Springs. She glanced over at his white button-down shirt crumpled on the floor.

Screw propriety. "Keep your eyes closed." She slipped her blouse over her head. At her command, Jack opened them instead.

"Holy—"

She shrieked and threw her arms over her chest, cutting him off mid-swear. "Close your eyes!"

"What are you doing?" He ignored her demand. His gaze was drawn to her bare skin like two bees to a vat of sweet honey.

In one ungraceful movement, she reached for Jack's discarded shirt and pressed it to her chest. "I said close your eyes."

Jack laughed. "Okay, they're closed."

She scrambled into his shirt.

"Jeez, Carrie," he said. "You'd think I never saw a naked woman before."

"I wasn't naked."

When Jack opened his eyes, Carrie was wearing his Armani dress shirt. "Did you see anything?" she asked, her arms swimming inside as she unclasped her bra. His shirt dwarfed her.

"You mean your pink bra with white lace around the edges? No, I didn't see it."

Carrie pulled the bra through her right sleeve and threw it at him. "You're real funny."

He lifted the piece of lingerie with his index finger and examined it. "34C. Very nice."

"Jack!"

He tossed it on top of their other clothing. "If you wanted to seduce me with sexy lingerie, you could have just asked."

"Do you have any idea how uncomfortable it is wearing that thing in this heat?" Carrie didn't add that the frivolous garment was a gift to herself from Victoria's Secret. Wearing sexy lingerie always gave her a big dose of self-confidence, and she had bought it for her meeting with Mr. Dillon. Unfortunately, the bra had been treating her breasts like pin cushions since the moment she put it on.

Jack undid his belt buckle and the hook of his tailored pants.

"Whoa." She jolted her hand forward. "What do you think you're doing?"

"Don't worry, I'm not taking them off."

"Darn right you're not."

His gaze flickered over her. "Relax. I'm just getting comfortable, too."

Carrie reconsidered, surveying his muscular form. She wouldn't mind seeing him without his pants. "Okay. You can take them off, but only if you're wearing boxers."

"I am wearing boxers," he informed her. "But I am still not taking off my pants."

She peered at him, curiosity piqued. "Why not?"

"Because."

"Because, why?" Carrie could not suppress a lighthearted smile. "Does your underwear have holes? Are they dirty? Didn't your mother ever warn you about not leaving the house without clean underwear?"

"My boxer shorts are in perfectly good condition, thank you very much."

"Then what?" Carrie's teasing smile broadened. "Is this a size thing? Are you ashamed of—"

"No!"

She laughed. "Then, what?"

Jack covered his mouth with his hand and mumbled something, turning away as he did.

"What?" She angled an ear toward him.

"I said I'm wearing Batman boxer shorts," he practically shouted.

Carrie burst out laughing, struggling to picture Batman boxer shorts on this man with the tailored suit and gold Rolex. She couldn't do it.

"Oh, take your pants off, if you're hot." Carrie giggled. "I won't tell anyone."

"I'd rather not. Do you have any idea how humiliating it would be if anyone ever saw me wearing Batman boxers?"

"Don't be a martyr. As soon as we hear the rescuers coming, you can put your pants back on and nobody will be the wiser." Carrie tried to be practical. "For now, just worry about staying cool."

Jack studied her for a moment with a quirky smile. "You're right." He eased out of his pants, and she bit her lower lip to keep from laughing at the black Batman logos scattered across his bright yellow boxer shorts. He folded the pants into a neat square and placed them on their growing pile of clothing in the corner of the elevator.

"When they find our bodies and see all these clothes on the floor, people will wonder what happened in here." Jack raised an eyebrow. "What will David think?"

"I don't care what David thinks." She pulled her sticky hair off her shoulders. "Besides, we won't be dead when they find us. Somebody must realize by now there are people stuck in here."

"Yes," Jack agreed, his voice turning sober. "But that only means they haven't been able to reach us yet."

His words sent a chill tingling along her spine. All this time, she'd assumed once Robert Dillon and his staff realized what had happened, help would be on the way. It never occurred to her receiving that help might be an impossibility.

Jack must have read the expression on her face as reality settled in. He took her hand in his and gave it a gentle pat. "Don't worry, sweetie. We'll be just fine." But his voice faded as he spoke the words, and his gaze dropped away.

"You don't think we're going to be rescued." Carrie's voice was as somber as the mood had grown.

"I don't know."

A hot sting of tears blurred her vision. Jack's strong arm came around her shoulders like a blanket of warmth, and she lowered her head to his chest. Her cheek pressed against the soft fabric of his white cotton undershirt, sending flutters rising within her. Carrie could hear his heart beating, feel her own pulse quickening with his touch. Was it possible in the midst of this disaster, Jack was experiencing the same attraction she was?

She pushed the thought away. Now was no time to be thinking about sex. But the idea loomed there, like an opportunity presenting itself, not to mention a welcome distraction given their predicament.

Lying in his embrace, she felt drugged by his manly scent—a sexy, sweaty scent mingled with the faint remnants of his cologne—and strangely content in his sheltering arms. His hand eased into the soft mass of her hair, and Carrie's arms tightened around him. She closed her eyes, absorbing his heat. Waiting.

For what, she wasn't sure.

Time dragged without compassion. She felt Jack swallow hard.

When he spoke, his voice was low and his breath hot against her skin. "Do you believe in fate?"

Carrie lifted her head to meet his gaze. Even in the darkness, she could see the intensity in his eyes. She breathed his name, and with his hand still engulfed in the cloud of her hair, he pulled her mouth to his.

Jack brushed his lips against hers, and her heartbeat quickened. She looked into his eyes, and then her lids fell shut. His mouth covered hers in a kiss as tender as a soft August breeze, tantalizing and sweet and a bit more persuasive than she cared to admit. He gathered her tingling body deeper into the circle of his arms.

"Carrie, Carrie." He whispered her name between kisses, caressing her with the words. His hands swept over her arms. "I feel as if I've known you forever. But I hardly know you at all."

She tipped her head back hungrily as he kissed her, her fingers diving into the thick dark hair above his collar. Flashes of light leaped across the horizon behind her closed eyelids as her body responded to his touch. They clung to each other, discovering the scents and textures and heat of each other's skin. Soft moans of passion escaped her throat as Jack's hand wandered through her hair and over the soft curve of her shoulder, down her arm, and finally onto her thigh.

It had been so long since a man held her like this. Carrie had almost forgotten what it was like to be at the mercy of her desires. She gave in to the pleasure his touch produced, all other thoughts fleeing from her mind. Like two wild animals, he ravaged her. And she willingly—eagerly—allowed herself to be ravaged.

Jack's hand slid along her thigh to the lace edges of her panties. Her back arched with a primal pleasure. She groaned and lifted her hips, urging him on. He pushed her panties to the side and slipped a finger inside of her.

Another moan escaped as his mouth crashed back upon hers. She tightened her grip around him. Jack's fingers quickened. Ripples of pleasure radiated from her core and surged through her body. She had never before experienced such desperate hunger for a man.

The time that had dragged just minutes ago now sped forward. Carrie didn't know how much of it they had left, but instinct told her not to waste a moment. The rhythmic movement of his fingers inside her cleared her mind of everything else. She was spinning, caught in the moment of sheer ecstasy.

Without realizing it was about to happen, she shuddered in his arms, calling his name, shocking even herself with the power of her orgasm. She clutched him harder as she came, holding on as she rode the wave of hot, pulsing pleasure as it overtook her body.

This is so fast, her common sense screamed. Too fast. Her eyes fluttered open. Control was not something she ever relinquished this easily. If she allowed her brain a moment to think straight, she would have been horrified. But then, how could she possibly think clearly with Jack's fingers still working their magic?

She slid her hand up his chest, feeling his taut muscles tighten beneath the thin undershirt. His hand captured hers and he raised it to his mouth. Carrie's gaze drifted to meet his smoldering eyes. He held her gaze with a deep intensity, brushing his lips across her fingertips with deliberate slowness, allowing her a moment to catch her breath.

She closed her eyes, enjoying the sensation. His tongue circled her fingers, sending fiery sparks through her entire body. She pulled her hand away reluctantly, and his lips reclaimed hers. Moving in unison, their entwined bodies drifted down until they were lying on the floor of the elevator. Jack rolled on top, pressing his full weight over her.

His tongue traced the edges of her lips, and she parted them, obedient to his unspoken demand. Carrie was crushed by his warmth, exhilarated by his touch. Never before had she felt so secure, so tempted.

"Oh, Jack." When he finally released her, she opened her eyes to find his face hovering mere inches above. Her fingers again disappeared into his hair. His hot breath stung her flesh as his tongue wandered, tracing the tender skin between her earlobe and collarbone.

She said his name again, feeling as if reality had ceased to exist and there was only the two of them, suspended somewhere beautiful between Heaven and Earth. His lips were magical, his voice intoxicating as he repeated her name between kisses, their two voices mingling in the darkened stillness. She could feel his hot length pressing against her as they rocked together on the floor.

Jack rolled over and pulled Carrie on top, his hands cupping her ass. "God, I could be with you forever," he whispered against her parted lips.

"Forever may not be very long for us."

"Forever is now."

"Jack…" Her head was drowning in the wave of passion that crashed over them. "This doesn't seem real. This can't be real."

He clasped her against him. "I don't know what's real anymore. All I know is you, Carrie. All I want is you. We may die here, but if I die, let it be in your arms."

"And if we live, let us be together forever."

"And never take life for granted again."

Jack sealed the vow with a kiss, his mouth claiming hers with wild desire. She lost herself in the embrace, her body swirling with the anticipation of making love to this man right here, right now. No precautions, no inhibitions—for tomorrow they may both be dead. But tonight, they were very much alive.

She dipped her hands under the waistband of his boxer shorts and grasped him eagerly. He was massive, and he was ready for her, long and hard and hot to the touch. Jack groaned as she explored his length with her hand, stroking him with her fingers. He was perfect.

When she could resist no longer, Carrie broke the kiss. Meeting his gaze for just a moment, she smiled, then took a deep breath and bent to taste him.

A loud sound grabbed her attention, and she stiffened and bolted upright. Her eyes widened and her skin bleached with fear.

"What is it?" At the sight of her reaction, Jack twisted from under her and sat up.

"Did you hear that?"

"Hear what?"

"Shh." Carrie clutched his forearm with an iron grip. "That…snapping…"

Jack rose to his feet and cocked an ear toward the ceiling. His impressive erection strained against the thin fabric of his boxer shorts. "I don't hear anything."

Before she could respond, the elevator plummeted. Jack's legs buckled from the force, and he crumbled to the floor beside her. She screamed, and he grabbed and pulled her close, clutching her body as they plunged to sure death.

The elevator shook with violent force as it bounced between the walls of the elevator shaft. Looking up through the open hatch, Carrie could see sparks flying as metal scraped against merciless metal. The raking sound intensified her screams. She sank her fingernails in the skin above Jack's elbow, and he grasped her tighter, but the pain was somehow exhilarating, reminding her they were both still alive.

Without warning, the elevator screeched to an abrupt halt. Jack's head cracked against the wall, and he cursed loudly. She bounced from his arms with the grace of a rag doll, landing on the floor in a heap of disarray.

The elevator eased down the remainder of the shaft, its doors opening with a *bing* as cheerful as if it had just made any average run from the nineteenth floor of the Grand Portofino Resort & Casino.

She threw up.

Still dizzy, she looked up. At least half a dozen people rushed toward them from the lobby. After spending the last several hours in a dark elevator, the bright lights were a shock. She squinted and shielded her eyes with a hand as she took in the chaos surrounding them.

Two paramedics were at her side in an instant, barraging her with questions. Several more surrounded Jack, and she watched helplessly as they eased him to his feet and out of the elevator.

Flashbulbs set the lobby ablaze as the media captured their exit from the elevator. Carrie gasped, stunned by the mass of people gathered behind the yellow police tape which blocked off the east bank of elevators. Reporters shouted questions and television cameras rolled, but all she could hear as the paramedics fussed around her were voices calling, "Mr. Dillon, Mr. Dillon!"

Trembling more from the chaos and confusion than from their five-hour ordeal, Carrie's eyes scanned the mass of people for Jack. At last, she caught a glimpse of his bright yellow Batman boxer shorts as he moved through the crowd.

She called his name from her perch on the stretcher where the paramedics had settled her, but he didn't appear to hear.

Sherry Winfield, the elegant African American marketing director for the Grand Portofino whom she had met in her New York office, approached with two men. Ignoring their presence, Carrie called Jack's name again. A paramedic attempted to examine her, but she brushed away his hand.

"Please," she implored. "He hit his head pretty hard. Please go check on Jack."

Sherry placed her hand on Carrie's shoulder. "Don't worry about Mr. Dillon, Carrie. He'll be well taken care of."

Carrie shook her head. Maybe she had bumped her head on the way down, too. "What do you mean, 'Mr. Dillon?'"

Sherry peered at her with concern. "Jack Dillon. Or Robert Dillon, as you probably know him. His personal physician is waiting to examine him in the office."

Chapter Three

Carrie lay curled under the covers of the king-size bed in her suite at the Grand Portofino, scrolling through her phone and listening to the lull of the television. Her mind was muddled as the adrenaline from their ordeal wore off, and she found herself unable to concentrate on either one. She was on the verge of drifting off when the voice of Bob Livingston, the eleven o'clock news anchorman, caught her attention.

"And in local news, blackjack wasn't the only gamble being taken at the new Grand Portofino Resort & Casino in Las Vegas. Electrical problems are being blamed for a situation which almost ended in tragedy tonight when an elevator lost power and stopped between floors with two people trapped inside. One of them was Robert Dillon, the hotel's owner.

"After several failed rescue attempts, experts tried to repair the faulty wiring, but inadvertently damaged the system, causing the elevator to plummet nineteen stories. Luckily, a safety device snapped into action at the last moment and both parties escaped with only minor injuries."

Carrie sat up in bed, watching the footage of Jack and her being helped from the elevator. She groaned when she saw her disheveled appearance. Her hair tousled every which way. Jack's oversized shirt hung well past the hem of her gray skirt, which was still hiked to her waist after their make-out session, causing it to look like she was wearing nothing at all underneath. Her hand had been shielding her eyes from the bright flashbulbs and camera lights, but seeing herself now on TV, it looked more like she'd been trying to hide her face from the cameras.

Pretty ironic, considering garnering media attention was the essence of her job as a public relations executive. But not like this.

"How freaking mortifying," she grumbled, resisting the urge to hurl her phone at the TV.

The camera angle switched to focus on Jack, and if Carrie hadn't been so mad at him for keeping his real identity a secret, she might now be sympathetic.

The cameras had zoomed right in on him, and even Bob Livingston couldn't resist a wisecrack as he appeared on screen, clad in his white undershirt and Batman boxer shorts. Jack ignored all attempts to be interviewed as his entourage led him through the mass of reporters. But she saw him glance back at the elevators. Had he been looking for her?

The footage cut to a headshot of Jack, dressed in a dark suit and tie. He looked incredibly debonair. She sighed and sank back against the pillow. Bob Livingston continued, "Robert Dillon made headlines in Las Vegas two years ago when he purchased the bankrupt Desert Star Hotel and announced plans to implode it and build a new hotel; what is now the Grand Portofino Resort & Casino. As we reported then, Dillon is no stranger to the business. This self-made billionaire has been making real estate deals and building hotels across the West Coast for fifteen years."

Carrie reached for the remote control and switched

off the television. She rolled onto her side and let her sleepless eyes drift to the window, the myriad of lights shining in from the Strip below a vibrant circus of color.

So Jack was Robert Dillon. Self-made billionaire. Owner of the Grand Portofino Resort & Casino.

Her potential client.

He was also a liar, Carrie reminded herself. She felt like such a fool. He'd known all along she was on her way to meet with "Mr. Dillon" and never once made an effort to clarify his identity. He had even looked at her presentation materials. The sample press releases. The social media campaign proposal. Carrie squeezed her eyes shut. How could he be so deceitful?

Was the passion between them one big lie, too?

Carrie grimaced into her pillow, realizing she had no one to blame but herself. If only she hadn't let her guard down.

Sliding deeper into the cool, soft sheets, she willed herself to forget about Jack Dillon. So they had shared a few steamy kisses, she reasoned, conveniently disregarding what else they had shared. It didn't change a thing. She had come to Las Vegas to pitch a potential client, and that was what she was going to do.

But try as she might, Carrie couldn't shake him from her consciousness. His image lingered in the room like a ghost. His strong hands. His sexy smile. The taste of his lips when they kissed. The way she quivered when he touched her. The words he had whispered.

Do you believe in fate?

She rolled onto her other side, turning her back to the window and all things Las Vegas. But the words still echoed in her mind, and when she at last fell asleep, Jack followed her into her dreams.

****

The next morning, Carrie rose with the desert sun, her body sore and temples throbbing. She swallowed two painkillers and settled into a hot bath to relax before her ten o'clock meeting with Jack and his leadership team.

Sherry had advised her of the rescheduled presentation time late last night when she called Carrie's suite to tell her Jack was doing fine; the bump on his head was minor and he didn't need stitches.

"I knew you were worried," Sherry explained. "Jack and our entire team are looking forward to your presentation tomorrow. If you're sure you are feeling up to it."

Carrie had thanked her and said she would be there, trying to sound grateful for the thoughtful gesture. After all, it wasn't Sherry's fault her boss was an egotistical liar. Carrie didn't mention Jack had already *seen* her presentation, sitting on the floor of the elevator last night after he inquired what was in the damaged Coach bag. That might have been a good time to tell her who he really was, before she had shown him her proposal and went on and on about wanting to impress "Mr. Dillon" with her presentation.

And now she had to see him again, face to face in front of Sherry and God knows who else. Instinct told her to pack her bags and get the hell out of town. Jump on the next plane to New York. She'd find an excuse for Phyllis.

Damn Jack. Carrie scowled, running the washcloth across her sore legs. She leaned back in the oval tub in the suite's grand bathroom. Damn Jack for making her think of returning to New York after all she'd gone through to get here. Damn him for shaking her confidence.

By nine thirty, Carrie's headache had subsided. She put on her best suit, styled her hair into a neat French twist, and applied her makeup. Then, after studying her appearance in the mirror, she pulled the pins from her hair and shook her head until the blonde waves tumbled down and fell below her shoulders.

"Fuck it. It's Vegas," she said to her reflection, giving her long hair one more run through with her fingers before heading to the elevator.

Although the resort's executive offices were located downstairs next to the Grand Portofino's expansive conference center, Jack kept his office in a suite on the thirtieth floor.

"He likes the view," Sherry had explained, when providing Carrie with directions on where to go when they spoke on the phone prior to her trip to Las Vegas.

She entered the suite and took a hard look around. The room was a departure from the hotel's Italian Riviera theme, decorated instead with steel-gray carpeting and black lacquer furnishings. A leather couch dominated the reception area, which was really the suite's living room. Above the couch, blueprints for the Grand Portofino were framed in silver. Unlike the rest of the hotel, Jack's executive offices lacked warmth; this room was cool, sleek, and void of a woman's touch, much like Jack Dillon himself.

Carrie approached the receptionist to introduce herself, but Sherry emerged from the hallway before she got the chance.

Dressed in an electric-blue dress that was somehow

both conservative and revealing, Sherry waved as she approached. "Carrie, we're ready for your presentation. How do you feel this morning?"

"I'm fine, thank you." She returned Sherry's smile. "A little sore."

Sherry looped her arm through Carrie's and led her through the door. The friendly gesture put Carrie at ease, and she understood why Sherry was Mr. Dillon's—*Jack's*—right-hand man.

"Mr. Dillon isn't feeling well himself this morning," Sherry told her. "I don't know if he'll be joining us."

Carrie's heart plummeted at the unexpected news. "He's not here?"

"No, but he asked us to proceed without him. Mr. Dillon is very eager to hire a new agency and get started. You're the last one to present."

"I see." *Chicken*. Carrie didn't need Jack's lame excuses to figure out why he really wasn't coming to the meeting.

"But he speaks very highly of you, so don't stress too much."

I'll just bet he does.

Sherry led her down a short hallway and into the conference room. Three people rose upon their entrance. "Carrie Thomas of Cresswell & Dailey Public Relations." Sherry introduced her. "This is Joan Watley, Associate Hotel Manager. Mark Jergens, Casino Manager, and Frank Giotto, Director of Food and Beverage."

Carrie shook hands and surveyed her potential clients. Mark Jergens was tall and slim, towering over her as he shook her hand. He had barely glanced her way when she walked into the room, but she felt certain he was studying her now, although his eyes were diverted. He was probably an eagle on the casino floor.

And Frank. With a name like Frank Giotto, Carrie would be certain he was a Vegas mob boss if she hadn't already known Jack owned the hotel. But with his dark features, graying temples, and conservative business suit, Frank looked more like The Godfather than a man who oversaw hotel restaurants.

Then there was Joan Watley, who looked more like she belonged in a ladies' clothing boutique than a conference room. With her impeccable dress, makeup, sleek hairstyle, and smug expression, she reminded Carrie of those snobby clerks who had asked Julia Roberts to leave their Rodeo Drive boutique in *Pretty Woman.*

Frank was the first to make the inevitable commentary. "Saw you on the eleven o'clock news last night. Not exactly the kind of publicity we were looking for, but you sure do know how to make a splash."

Laughter rippled around the table.

Mark couldn't resist adding, "Next time you get the Grand Portofino on the news, try to publicize something other than our faulty wiring."

Carrie shot him a wry smile, annoyed by how her potential clients found the situation funny. It was rare for hotel executives—particularly a brand spanking new hotel—to find humor in the fact that two people were almost killed on their premises.

"I agree, Mr. Jergens." She shifted into all-business mode. As if she had flipped a magic switch, the laughter ceased, and all eyes turned in her direction.

She rose and stood behind her chair, gaining

confidence as her audience was forced to look up at her. Standing allowed her authority and the appearance of power, and it gave her the freedom to move around.

"First of all," she began, "how did the media even get inside the building during a crisis? Who allowed TV cameras to assemble right there in the elevator bank when you had no idea what the visual would be once those doors opened? You could have had two dead bodies on the news last night." She paused for effect and was rewarded with their duly admonished expressions. "If Cresswell & Dailey comes on board, that kind of negligence stops right now."

There, she had said the thing bothering her most since watching the news on TV last night. And now she definitely had their undivided attention. Energy surged through her body; she was in her element, and it felt amazing.

"Obviously, we don't want people to associate the Grand Portofino with danger or inadequacy." As she spoke, the gears in Carrie's mind sprang into action. New ideas began spinning through her head, and before she could even think them through, they were escaping her lips. "The key is to acknowledge the elevator incident, but then move on. Focus on positive things. Joan, has the problem been fixed?"

Joan raised an eyebrow. "They're working on it this morning." Her reply was speculative. Carrie could tell she'd be a tough one to win over.

"Good. We'll distribute a press release announcing a full inspection and highlight state-of-the-art safety features throughout the hotel. The safety of our guests is the Grand Portofino's number one priority," she added for emphasis.

Carrie began pacing, so excited she almost forgot where she was and who she was speaking to. This was the part of her job she loved, the on-the-spot challenge that got her creative juices flowing. "Then, we develop a great promotion. Of course, we'll have the traditional press releases and media tours, but we need one big idea to wow the world. Something that will get the media excited and forget all about the elevator incident. Something Las Vegas has never seen before."

"Believe me," Joan interjected, her words as sour as her pinched expression, "this town has seen it all."

"What's new and different?" Carrie asked the group, not allowing the other woman's negative attitude to stand in her way.

Sherry turned to Mark, who was seated beside her at the long glass conference room table. "Everything in the casino is brand new and state of the art. Didn't you say those digital slot machines were the latest and greatest?"

"All of the casinos have them now," Mark said.

"Besides"—she reached for her battered Coach tote—"we want something universally appealing. Despite its reputation, not everyone comes to Las Vegas to gamble."

Mark said, "Slots account for a huge percentage of the casino's revenue."

Carrie opened her planner and flipped through to the notes she had taken during their previous meeting in New York. "Sherry, didn't you mention something about a celebrity chef coming to the Grand Portofino?"

Frank answered for her. "Yes, Antonio Cardini is opening a new, very upscale Italian restaurant here at the hotel. He runs a chain in New York and across the

East Coast."

"And when will he be here?"

"Two weeks from Monday. Cardini's opens in three weeks, and he'll be here the week prior for final preparations and to shoot a commercial."

"Okay." Carrie tapped her fingers against the glass tabletop, considering the possibilities. "Three weeks, three weeks…" she mused aloud, contemplating the options. She did not hear the door open behind her, nor did she see the tall figure slip into the conference room.

"Okay, here's what we do." The room pulsed with anticipation as she spoke. "I'll need all the information on Antonio Cardini you've got. I'll put together a special press kit, including a bio of Cardini and photos of the restaurant, sample menus…whatever you can get me. We'll plan a grand opening—a huge press event—invite all key media from the most important magazines and websites, give them a wonderful meal and let them review it…"

"What about the ideas we discussed at our meeting in New York?" Sherry asked.

"Oh yes, those ideas." She thought back to the lack of enthusiasm Jack had expressed when she shared her proposal in the elevator last night. She pulled five copies of the document from her bag and passed them out. With a broad smile illuminating her face, Carrie announced her next proposal. "Rip it up."

"Excuse me?" Joan surveyed Carrie with narrowed eyes, as if she suggested they all take their clothes off.

"I said rip it up. Those ideas are old news, dull, probably the same things you've heard from every other agency who has done a pitch. Go on, tear them to pieces."

Just for effect, she snatched Frank's copy of the proposal and proceeded to tear it to shreds, tossing bits of paper into the air as she did. They drifted to the table and her feet like plump snowflakes.

All eyes fixed upon her, clearly amused by Carrie's unusual command and not at all taking her seriously. Frank crossed his arms and leaned back in his chair, a quirky smile tugging his lips.

"What the Grand Portofino needs is innovation. Fresh ideas. Set ourselves apart from the other hotels on the Strip."

"An excellent plan, Ms. Thomas." Jack's voice boomed. "Not at all what we discussed last night, but then I never was too keen on your agency's idea to host a 'Gamble for Charity' event in my casino."

Carrie whirled around to find Jack advancing toward her. She must have done so in an awkward way because the underwire in her bra poked through the sheer fabric and jammed her quite unmercifully in the tender spot just beneath her armpit.

"Excuse me, *Mr. Dillon*." Carrie's eyes burned into him, the jolt from the underwire adding to her displeasure. "I didn't hear you come in. I trust you're feeling better?" She kept her voice cool beyond formal.

"I am, thank you," he returned, easing into the black leather swivel chair at the head of the table. Jack was dressed in an impeccable dark navy suit, yet Carrie immediately saw him as he was last night. Near naked and sexy and sweating from more than just the heat of the stopped elevator. Her face flared with embarrassment, and she hoped the redness wasn't creeping across her skin.

Jack stared back at her. "Please, continue with your

proposal. I'm intrigued."

She turned, trying to compose herself and hold on to the gusto developing their new PR plan had lit within her. But there was no ignoring the chemistry between them and being this close to the man who had made her scream with pleasure mere hours ago was knocking her off her game.

She also couldn't ignore the sharp pierce of the protruding underwire cutting into her skin. Victoria had finally revealed her secret. Never wear a push-up bra to an important presentation.

Carrie cleared her throat. "As I was saying—"

"Brilliant!" Jack slammed a commanding palm against the table. "You're hired. Congratulations, Carrie." He rose, extending his hand.

"But, Jack, I—" Carrie reached to shake his hand, but as she raised her arm, the underwire poked her again. She flinched and pulled her hand away.

He looked perplexed by her behavior, but before he could question it, Joan stood. "Mr. Dillon, we have several agencies still under consideration. I don't think we should make rash decisions based merely on Ms. Thomas's ambitious ideas."

Jack held his hand forward in protest, silencing her. "There's no better idea than an ambitious one."

Carrie refused to satisfy him with any show of gratitude. Instead, she began dispensing orders to the group. Jack leaned back in his chair at the head of the conference room table, watching her with an expression of sheer admiration.

"Well, it's all settled then," she said. "I'll have my office send a contract to you, Mr. Dillon. We'll also have to find time to talk about the budget."

She turned to Frank. "I'll need to get all the pertinent information from you to include in the press releases. You have information on Antonio Cardini's schedule?"

He nodded. "Yeah, whatever you need."

"Good," Carrie said. "And we'll need to discuss the logistics of the press event, too. Do you have time to give me a tour this afternoon? I'd like to decide where the musicians and the podium will go."

"Whoa, whoa, whoa." Frank rose from his chair. "I'm all for this media blitz idea of yours, but musicians?" He snickered and addressed the others still seated. "Next thing you know she'll want dancing bears and superheroes entertaining the guests."

Jack's eyes narrowed as he leaned across the table toward Frank. His reflection on the glass tabletop was as imposing as the man himself. "Do you have a problem with superheroes?"

Frank stopped short, realizing his mistake. Then he grinned. "No, sir." Everyone at the table smiled, but Carrie treated herself to a chuckle at the obvious reference to Jack's now-infamous Batman boxer shorts.

Jack glanced in Carrie's direction at the sound of her laughter, his smile broadening with her candid response. With his eyes still locked on hers, he said, "I'm wearing Iron Man today, so let's not hear any Avengers cracks, either."

She still had a list of tasks to assign, but before she could continue, Jack clapped his powerful hands together. "Let's get to work."

All four members of his senior leadership team sprang into action, and moments later, she was alone in the room with Jack. Dismayed, she avoided looking at him, turning her attention instead to her abandoned presentation materials still spread around the table.

The upbeat façade she had embodied during the meeting dissolved as she gathered her belongings. She felt Jack's eyes settle on her, as if waiting for her to speak. Waiting for her to turn to him with the adoring eyes she had had last night.

But hell if that was going to happen.

When she finally did turn around, her eyes were cold. "Why didn't you tell me who you were last night?"

Her question seemed to surprise him. "I didn't want you to feel intimidated by me."

She raked him with a frosty glare. "I don't get intimidated, *Robert*."

He moved toward her, but the venomous look she shot stopped him from coming any closer. "You knew who I was the whole time we were in the elevator and never once thought it might be pertinent to mention you were the guy I was on my way upstairs to meet?"

"I was going to tell you."

"When?" Carrie demanded. "After you fucked me, or after the elevator crashed and we were both dead?"

Jack winced at her words. "It's not like that. I never meant to mislead you."

"Mislead me?" She didn't even attempt to hide the bitter edge in her voice. Did he even hear what he was saying? "You lied to my face."

"I did not lie." His words were measured but still held a defensive tone. Then his lip twitched upward. "I never said I *wasn't* Robert Dillon."

"That's not fucking funny." Carrie slammed her papers on the table. The wild unleashing of her anger surprised even her. Two f-bombs in under a minute—to a client nonetheless—was not her usual style. Something about this man unraveled her in every possible way. "And why the hell do you go by 'Jack' anyway?"

"I go by my middle name with people I know personally."

"You don't know me at all."

"Robert sounds so formal," he explained. "And somehow, going by the name 'Bob Dillon' never seemed like a good idea."

"Bob Dylan spells his name different."

"Carrie." Jack placed a hand on her shoulder, but she yanked it away, cursing the underwire as it stabbed her again. "Would it help if I apologized?"

"It would be a start."

"I gave you the account, didn't I?"

"You didn't give me anything," she said, her voice rising again. "I earned it."

"I didn't have to hire you."

"Oh, Jack." Carrie shook her head as if he were the most pathetic thing she'd ever laid eyes on. "We're both intelligent people, so let's not humor each other. I didn't flee town last night when I found out who you are because I know how important this account is to my agency. And you hired us because you know I'm the best damn publicist you'll ever find. So let's just put the past behind us and get on with business."

"What about last night?" Jack challenged.

That was a tough one. True, he had deceived her, but she couldn't erase what had happened between them in the elevator. The smell of Jack's cologne triggered memories of his kisses, his touch, the way his skin had scraped against hers. The man radiated sensuality. She could not deny her attraction to him.

But it had all been an illusion.

She shook away the lustful sensation rippling up her spine and looked him in the eye, summoning all the reason she had within her. "Last night we thought we were about to die."

"That doesn't mean anything."

"It means *everything*," Carrie insisted. "We were two different people than we are now. We were strangers, feeling sorry for ourselves and grateful for each other's company, and one thing naturally led to another. But now we're back in the real world where you are Robert Dillon—my client—and there's work to be done. So let's pretend last night never happened and move on."

Jack looked as if he was about to argue her textbook assessment, and she didn't want to hear it. Before he could say a word, she added, "And another thing. I'd appreciate it if you didn't tell anyone what happened in that elevator."

"Why would I tell anyone?"

"You seem like the type of man who likes to brag." Carrie finished gathering her papers and turned to face him. "I wouldn't want anyone to think I got this account because…" She gestured at the space between them.

"Don't flatter yourself." Jack let out a bitter laugh. "Do you really think I'd brag to my colleagues like some horny teenager? Like you said, the account is yours because you earned it."

"I'm just laying the ground rules." She threw her arms in the air. "I don't know why you're getting defensive. I'm the one who should be mad."

"So be mad."

Carrie slumped into Jack's chair at the head of the table. "This is crazy. The last thing we should be doing is fighting."

He stared at her, his face an unreadable mask, like the poker players in the casino thirty stories below.

"We have to put last night behind us," Carrie said after a few moments had passed. Her words were strong and resolute. "That's the only way this will work."

"Is that really what you want?"

Carrie folded her arms across her chest. What she wanted was for him to take her downstairs to her suite and pick up where they were interrupted in the elevator the night before. No, wait. What she wanted to do was travel back in time and erase what had happened between them altogether.

But that didn't feel right either.

Carrie sighed. She couldn't change the past. She couldn't change the fact they had shared one of the most intense, passionate moments of her life. That Jack had touched her in places she still blushed to think about. They had been prepared to die together, and in that state of mind, let go of all inhibitions and thrown common sense to the wind.

"That's how it has to be." She forced herself to meet his probing gaze. "Last night was a mistake, Jack, plain and simple. We are just going to have to move on."

He leaned in far closer than necessary. Electricity tingled between them. "You can think last night was a mistake if you want to, but this isn't over," he informed her, his breath hot on her skin. "Not by a long shot."

She took a step back, barely able to maintain her balance as his words and the blazing impact of his nearness hit her. She had to get away if she had any shot in hell of keeping her wits intact.

"I'm going to catch a flight back to New York this afternoon," she said, struggling to hold on to her composure. "Why don't we schedule a conference call with Phyllis Dailey for first thing tomorrow morning?"

Jack smiled as if the devil had possessed him. "I don't think so."

"Excuse me?"

"Oh, plan the conference call with Phyllis," he said. "But you'll be on my side of the line."

"Jack…" Carrie's warning had all the warmth of a grizzly bear's growl.

"I think you'd be much more productive working at the hotel, at least until the day of this big Cardini event you have cooking. No pun intended."

"You can't be serious."

"Let me put it this way," he said. "I am hiring Cresswell & Dailey to handle PR for this hotel on one condition. That you spend the next three weeks working on-site at the Grand Portofino."

"This is ludicrous!" Carrie exploded. "This is blackmail."

"Uh-uh." Jack waggled a finger at her, his mischievous smile widening. "Never argue with the client."

Chapter Four

Jack tapped his fingers on the steering wheel as he headed home from work, driving on autopilot; his racing thoughts made it impossible to focus on the road. Two days ago, his life had been exactly where he wanted it. He worked every day and was content with putting one hundred percent of his energy into building his business. No complications, no romantic entanglements. Nothing to interrupt his plans. And that was the way he liked it.

Until *she* walked into his life.

Jack replayed their conversation in his mind. She was a spitfire, no doubt about it. But her angst was not unjustified. In fact, he deserved every word she had fired at him.

His lip twitched into a smile. If he was being totally honest, he was guilty as sin for egging her on. He couldn't help it though. Listening to her rake him over the coals, green eyes on fire, and curse words spewing from her pretty little mouth was a huge turn on. Nobody ever dressed him down the way Carrie did in the conference room today. Just thinking about it again made his dick stir to life, right there in the driver's seat of his Audi.

Maybe he should have been straight and mentioned he owned the hotel, but damn it, he was attracted to her. Too many women in the past had thrown themselves at him because he was Jack Dillon, billionaire. But by the time Jack had realized she was on her way to his office to do a PR pitch, it was too late to set the record straight.

When she announced she was heading back to New York, it hit him like a punch in the stomach. He couldn't stand the idea of her leaving Las Vegas. Not yet, when she still thought he was a first-class asshole, and last night was the mistake of a lifetime. Of all the words in the English language, "regret" was the last one he wanted her to associate with him.

His chagrin grew deeper now with the realization Carrie wanted nothing to do with him.

As he waited at a stoplight, Jack tried to convince himself it was for the best. Sure, it might be nice to have a little romance in his life, but the Grand Portofino had just opened, and the next couple of months would be a whirlwind of activity. He had meetings with investors, appointments with inspectors, and now this restaurant opening was shaping up to be a big to-do. It was going to take all his time and energy to meet his business obligations.

All of which added up to one hard truth. The last thing he needed in his life was a woman to distract him.

So be it.

Feeling a little better, Jack pulled through the gates of the private residential community where he lived. It was seven thirty, which meant he had just enough time to shower, change, and grab something to eat. He wanted to make it back to the Grand Portofino by nine o'clock for the casino's busiest hours. He would spend an hour or two there and then visit a few of the other casinos on the Strip to see how their business was doing. It was a ritual he followed at least once or twice a week.

His house was in a new development, its light tan façade nestled among the desert palms and cacti, which lined the freshly paved streets of one of Las Vegas's most exclusive neighborhoods. His home overlooked a rolling green golf course, but he didn't play. In fact, Jack found the sport painfully boring. But he liked the view and the privacy afforded being adjacent to the golf course.

Driving through the serene neighborhood was still a novelty; he had moved in a few months ago. He made it a habit to keep a home and car in every city where he owned a hotel. He had spent the early years of his success living in the hotels themselves, but it didn't take him long to tire of the impersonal lifestyle. He hated the lack of privacy and missed having room to spread out.

Jack owned properties in California, Arizona, and now Nevada, but lately, he'd been spending most of his time in Las Vegas. He planned to make Las Vegas home base from here on out and travel to his other properties only when necessary. He had his eye on another Vegas hotel, too. Las Vegas was growing nonstop, and all his business instincts told him to focus his energies there.

He pulled the Audi into his driveway but didn't open the garage. He'd be leaving again soon. Instead, he walked up the short, landscaped pathway to his front door.

Disarming the security system in his front entry, he thought of his brother, Doug, living with his wife and daughters in their modest three-bedroom ranch outside of Toledo. Jack had offered them money, offered his brother a job managing any of his hotels in any city he wanted, but Doug Dillon was never interested. Doug preferred his average life with his average job and average house, and as Jack entered his own empty house, he would have traded every dollar he ever earned to experience the love and contentment Doug took for granted. To have a wife greet him at the door with a kiss and a beer the way Amanda did for Doug, now that was worth millions.

He trudged across the living room and withdrew a bottle of scotch from the liquor cabinet. Now, why the hell was he thinking about crazy things like kids and marriage?

It was that damn Carrie Thomas and her form-fitting business suits. He took a long swallow of scotch. Hadn't he just resolved to stop thinking about her?

Maybe his mind was stuck on her because they had come so close to what promised to be mind-blowing sex, and then he was left hanging. The cold shower afterward didn't do much to ease his frustration, either.

He took another sip of his scotch. Who was he kidding? The reason he couldn't shake Carrie from his system had nothing to do with sex. After their night of spilling secrets in the elevator, his connection to her stretched so much deeper. It was kind of crazy to think how fast she'd gotten under his skin.

He'd been working his ass off for years. Sure, he'd had his share of flings and one-nighters, but with no steady relationship to distract him from business, he was able to eat, sleep, breathe his hotels.

But more and more—though he cringed to admit it—the notion of a more conventional lifestyle crept into his mind. Owning successful hotels and having lots of money and power were only fulfilling to a point. What he craved was what his brother possessed. He wanted a wife whom he could love and trust and respect and make love to without having to second-guess her motives. And yes, he even wanted kids.

At the moment though, those things seemed far beyond his grasp. Jack couldn't help but sigh at the sad irony. So the old saying was true after all; money can't buy happiness.

He finished his drink and ambled into the kitchen to put the empty scotch glass in the sink. He allowed himself one drink a day. Just one, whether it be at a business dinner or nights like tonight when he needed to slow his brain down for a minute. Staying sharp and in control was as necessary as having air to breathe.

He went upstairs to hop in the shower, thoughts returning to Carrie. What was it about her that had him reexamining his entire value system? In two days, she had managed to shake his entire world to its core.

And he didn't like it. Not one bit.

****

"You did what?" Carrie held the phone away from her ear as Phyllis Dailey reacted to her confession. She could almost picture Phyllis sinking onto the plush sofa in her Greenwich Village apartment as Carrie rehashed the events of last evening.

"I'm sorry, Phyl." Carrie leaned against the glass of the floor-to-ceiling window in her suite at the Grand Portofino, looking out at the lights on the Vegas Strip. The sidewalks were already crowded with people, drifting from casino to casino in the early hours of the evening. Carrie frowned into the phone. "I didn't want to tell you at all, but I just had to tell somebody."

"What were you thinking, Carrie?"

"I didn't know it was him. He knew I was on my way to meet 'Mr. Dillon.' He went out of his way not to tell me who he really was. You know I would have never let anything happen if I had known."

Phyllis's laughter was rich and genuine. "No, my dear, you would have taken the opportunity to pitch the account right there and then. That's why I sent you to Las Vegas, Carrie; you're not afraid to take the bull by the horns."

Carrie smiled at her boss's compliment. This was the second time today the two women had spoken. Carrie and Jack had called Phyllis together from his office, and she was appropriately thrilled to learn Carrie had landed the account for Cresswell & Dailey, and more than happy to agree to overnight all of her files and the personal items she requested to the hotel.

"So you're not mad because I almost slept with our client?" Carrie asked now, cringing at the words she never in a million years could have imagined having to utter. She was eager to end this part of their conversation.

"Just don't let Jim find out," Phyllis warned. Jim Cresswell was the other half of Cresswell & Dailey. Older, more conservative, and no way as open-minded as Phyllis, Jim would never approve of an affair between an employee and a client, even if it was technically by accident.

If Jim ever got wind of what had happened with Jack, any shot she might have at becoming a partner in the agency would be gone. Heck, she'd be lucky if she got to keep her job at all.

"You remember what happened to Gina Dixon, don't you?" Phyllis said. "Three years with the agency as an account executive, until Jim found out she was messing around with a client. He had her ordering office supplies and fetching coffee until she was so bored, she quit. It was the best thing she could have done for herself, anyway. Her upward mobility at C & D was pretty much cooked."

"I remember." Carrie groaned, sinking into the armchair in the suite's living room. She and Gina had been close friends when both worked for the agency. Phyllis didn't know it, but Gina had confided in Carrie about the affair long before Jim Cresswell found out. They'd been pretty good about keeping things a secret until one night Jim showed up at the office after-hours and caught the two of them horizontal on the conference room table. Last she heard, Gina had moved home to New Jersey and was working at a car dealership in Hackensack.

She was not about to let her own career meet the same fate. She needed to put Jack Dillon out of her mind for good. "About the account, Phyllis..."

Phyllis listened while Carrie detailed the new plan to promote Cardini's and the celebrity chef. Antonio Cardini was a regular on several cable television cooking shows, known around the world for his trendy restaurants and mouth-watering recipes. He was a demanding businessman, a perfectionist in the kitchen, and he loved the media's attention. As the public relations agency for Jack's hotel, it was her job to make sure he got it.

Together, she and Phyllis hammered out a media plan and discussed the details of the account in preparation for their conference call with Jack in the morning.

"You know," Phyllis said, tapping her pen so hard Carrie could hear it on her end of the line, "I think this might end up being one of the best campaigns we've ever done."

Pride rippled over her. Phyllis didn't normally approve of important client decisions being made without her, but Carrie knew her boss respected her professional judgment and understood the importance of knowing when to change course on the fly. She was glad Phyllis was pleased with the new plan.

"So what are your plans for tonight?" Phyllis asked, now that they were finished discussing business. "Roulette? Blackjack? Not a rendezvous with our friend Mr. Dillon, I hope."

"No, Phyllis, I think things would be best if I kept my distance from him outside of work." Carrie rose from the armchair and peered again through the window. The night was dark now, the air pulsing with an electric energy only Las Vegas could produce. From her vantage point, she could see the dazzling entrance to the MGM Grand and the Statue of Liberty rising before the New York-New York Hotel & Casino.

"I'm going out tonight," she told Phyllis, the words an alluring promise on her lips. The glamour of the city at night beckoned her, quickening her pulse with a sharp eagerness to see the sights. "You know, check out the client's competition. Take a look at some of the other hotels on the Strip."

"I hope you brought something decent to wear." Dressing accordingly was always a priority to Phyllis.

Carrie smiled into the phone, thinking of the new

clothes hanging in her closet. "I guess Jack felt guilty about holding me hostage at his hotel for three weeks, so he sent me to the shops on the concourse to buy whatever I needed for my stay. I spent the afternoon shopping."

"You bought a nice dress, I assume."

Carrie laughed. "Try three. Plus several suits, a pair of jeans, three pairs of shoes, and a month's worth of lingerie."

Phyllis sucked in her breath. "Please tell me you're kidding."

"Oh, no. Jack Dillon owes me, and he owes me big time. You know, Christian Dior has amazing clothes."

"Carrie—"

"Don't worry. Jack can afford it," Carrie said, waving her hand. "Besides, I'm sure it's a business expense. He just told me to charge everything to the room."

"If you get this agency fired because of your expensive shopping spree…"

"Trust me on this one." She smiled. "Jack isn't going to say a word about it."

Phyllis sighed, and Carrie could tell she was unconvinced. "Well, just remember, you can't charge poker chips to your room."

"You know I don't gamble, Phyl." Carrie's voice was firm and final. "And I *don't* get involved with my clients."

****

Half an hour later, Carrie took the elevator to the lobby, dressed in a tight but tasteful black dress and new high heels. She bypassed the Grand Portofino's casino and went outside. She didn't want to risk running into Jack again until absolutely necessary.

The hot air hit her like a blast from an open oven as she stepped outside onto Las Vegas Boulevard. Even at night, the temperature hovered at ninety degrees.

The street buzzed with energy. Tourists drifted from one casino to the next. She spent the evening exploring the various hotels in the area, jotting notes in the planner she always carried in her bag. When she had toured the MGM Grand, Mandalay Bay, and Park MGM casinos, she took a taxi to the other end of the Strip and began checking those hotels, as well.

The casinos were packed with people. Overweight old ladies with tee shirts boasting "Las Vegas, Nevada" or "The Grand Canyon" sat along rows of slot machines, looking more transfixed than entertained as they fed bills into the machines. Groups of twentysomethings dressed to the nines waited in line to get into nightclubs, and music from the various live lounge acts radiated through the casino floors.

By eleven o'clock, Carrie was exhausted from being on her feet all evening. Against the monotonous singsong of the slot machines and loud music, she eased onto a barstool at the Bellagio and ordered a glass of wine.

"Fourteen dollars." The bartender raised his voice above the hum of the casino, placing the Chardonnay in front of her.

Before Carrie could reach for her purse, a man's hand slipped past her with a twenty-dollar bill. "Keep the change."

The bartender took the bill and walked away. She followed the hand from its hairy knuckles and abundant silver jewelry to the face it was attached to.

"Thanks." She turned back to the row of liquor bottles lining the wall behind the bar and took a sip of wine, hoping he would go away.

Instead of leaving, he hopped onto the vacant barstool beside her. "Name's Drew Hollingsworth." His voice was tinged with the South, and the words rolled off his tongue with as much sensuality as if he'd said, "Make love to me, Carrie Thomas."

His gaze trailed up her long, crossed legs. He wasn't looking at her face when he added, "From Swainsboro, Georgia."

Carrie turned to him with a smug expression on her face. She had spent enough time in New York City bars to know when an over-confident—and probably married—creep was hitting on her. This one was particularly unpleasant, from the chest hair springing from beneath his collar to his sour breath. The smell hit her, and she winced. She'd bet a million dollars he'd been in the casino all night, drinking the free alcohol casino cocktail waitresses hustled twenty-four hours a day.

"Shame you Georgia boys don't carry toothbrushes," she drawled in an exaggerated Southern accent.

His broad smile revealed the cockiest set of pearl-white teeth Carrie had ever seen. He didn't even catch on she was mocking him. "Left it back home, with my wife."

"How nice." Carrie hid her smirk behind another sip of the Chardonnay and turned away. Why were men so damn predictable?

Drew placed a hand on her knee. "So what's a pretty girl like you doing here all by yourself?"

"Leaving, now." Carrie placed her unfinished wineglass on the bar and stood.

Drew caught her by the wrist and pulled her ear close to his mouth. The smell of booze rumbled over her as he spoke. "Hey, baby, what's your rush? I got a room upstairs. What do you say?" He exposed a folded hundred-dollar bill and rubbed it between his thumb and forefinger.

She yanked her arm from his grip and shot him a hostile glare. "Do I look like a damn hooker?"

"I got a hundred bucks says you do tonight."

Carrie retrieved her wineglass from the bar and splashed its contents onto his face. He jumped from the stool and took a swing at her. Several people around the bar turned to observe the spectacle.

"Slut!" he hollered, missing.

Disgusted by the insult, she lunged at him with all the might her petite frame possessed. But she was caught midair around the waist by a powerful arm. She shrieked in surprise as her body swung out of Drew's reach and set down on the floor.

She didn't need to see his face to know it was Jack Dillon standing between her and Drew Hollingsworth. Even from behind, she recognized him in an instant. His broad shoulders loomed before her. He stood tall and tense, dressed in a gray suit and shiny black shoes, fists clenched by his sides. Beside him, Drew looked skinny and powerless.

"You want to start something?" Jack asked, his voice a fierce growl.

"Who the hell asked you to butt in?" Drew demanded, wiping the wine from his face with a cocktail napkin. "This is between me and the little whore."

Jack popped him in the face.

Carrie gasped as Drew stumbled backward. He grabbed the lip of the bar to keep from falling to the floor. Regaining his balance, he raised a hand to his nose. When he moved it a moment later, it was covered in blood.

"I'll say it again." Jack raised his fist. "Do you want to start something?"

Drew looked from Jack to Carrie and back to Jack. He dismissed them both with a sweep of his hand and walked away.

Jack turned to her, his eyes hard and jaw set tight. She had never seen such a cold expression on such an otherwise attractive face. It didn't suit him at all, and Carrie couldn't understand why he was aiming his angry gaze her way.

"A pleasure, as always." He glowered at her and turned away.

Carrie released the breath caught in her throat. "What are you doing here?"

He began to stomp through the crowd, but she followed. Over his shoulder, Jack spat, "Saving your life. I didn't realize when I hired your agency, I'd be paying you to get drunk and pick bar fights."

"Get drunk and pick bar fights?" Carrie repeated in disbelief. The blood flowed through her veins like lava scalding the Earth. "For your information, I am not drunk, and I was not picking a bar fight. And by the way, *Mr. Dillon*, I wouldn't be in this seedy little town at all if you hadn't decided to hold me…" She struggled to contain herself, groping for the proper word to express her frustration. "Hostage! Remember that next time you start throwing around nasty accusations."

"I call it like I see it." Jack quickened his stride. "Just be glad I stepped in when I did."

"Hey, nobody asked you to step in at all," she said. "I can take care of myself."

"I can tell. Another minute I'd be scraping you off the floor of the Bellagio."

"You forget I'm from New York," she said, rifled by his arrogance. "Handling drunken losers is part of the territory."

"Is putting yourself at risk to get beaten, raped, or even murdered part of the territory, too?"

Carrie thought about it for a moment, then smiled. "As a matter of fact, it is."

Jack stopped. "Oh," he said, glancing her way. "I guess you're right."

Carrie stayed at his side as they began walking again. They made their way through the crowded casino and passed through the hotel's entrance to the outside. Jack placed a protective hand on the small of her back as they crossed the driveway, where the Bellagio's signature attraction greeted them. Dozens of people lined the sidewalk overlooking the lake, where the fountains would soon spring to life.

Curiosity led Carrie to join the crowd, and Jack stopped beside her. He checked his watch. "I think it's about to start."

"Oh, good," she exclaimed, a wave of excitement sweeping over her. "I've always wanted to see this."

"Let's watch it from the front." Jack placed a hand on the small of her back and led the way. The sweet smell of the flowers growing along the walkway calmed her, and she breathed it in. They made it to Las Vegas

Boulevard just as the fountains rose from the water.

Planting her hands on the rail, she looked around in fascination as the lake illuminated with dancing water and light, mesmerizingly choreographed to the croon of Frank Sinatra singing "Fly Me to the Moon." The elegant Bellagio Hotel tower rose high above the fountains, creating a breathtaking backdrop, and across the street at the Paris Las Vegas Hotel & Casino, the lights of the soaring Eiffel Tower blinked in sync to the music.

"Oh, it's so beautiful," she said. The whole boulevard sprang to life. As they watched the show, she was wholly aware of Jack standing beside her. He was a magnificent presence, so tall and good-looking. She was drawn to him like a magnet to steel, and the intense glances he kept shooting her way told her he felt the attraction, too.

By the time the show neared its finale and the water shot into the sky, Carrie's heartbeat had crescendoed right along with the music. She was breathless as Frank sang the final notes of the song, and the show concluded with an explosion of water and light. She joined the other spectators in an enthusiastic round of applause.

Jack nudged her arm and led her away as the crowd started to shift. Without a word, they crossed the street back toward the Grand Portofino. Their hands brushed, sending forbidden sparks straight up Carrie's arm. Jack must have felt them too, because he buried his hands in the pockets of his trousers.

After a few moments of silence, she asked, "So what *are* you doing on this end of town?"

"I try to visit some of the other hotels on the Strip

at least once a week. See how they're doing. What are you doing over here?"

"Same," Carrie said. "Comparison shopping."

"For what?"

"For you." Her glance swept his way. "To see how the Grand Portofino measures up."

Jack stepped aside to let Carrie squeeze through a throng of tourists on the street, and as they moved single file through the crowd, his protective hand landed firmly on her shoulder. She angled her head to look at Jack's hand and then glanced up to his face. But instead of meeting his gaze, she found his eyes cast downward, staring at her ass. The discovery sent another little thrill bolting through her, and she was glad she wore her new black dress. Let him look at what he can't touch. With a smirk, she turned and kept moving forward.

As soon as they passed through the crowd, he quickened his stride and returned to her side. "So how am I doing so far?"

"Doing? With what?"

He smiled, dropping the hand from her shoulder. "With my hotel. You said you were comparison shopping."

"Right." She could still feel the burn of his eyes on her body and the tingle on her shoulder where his hand had rested. "Okay."

"Just okay?" Jack's eyebrows shot up in surprise.

"Well—" She measured her words."—you're off to a strong start, but we really need to wow people to keep the momentum going."

He motioned for her to continue.

"The Bellagio has the fountains, The Venetian has

the canals, and almost everywhere has roller coasters or similar attractions. The Grand Portofino is beautiful, but it needs some extra oomph."

"Are you suggesting I build a roller coaster? Maybe run it right through the casino past the roulette tables?" he asked, his voice incredulous. "The whole idea of the Grand Portofino is it's a classy place for classy people. I don't want to be another Circus Circus with kids running around everywhere and juggling acts distracting people from the casino floor."

"Your resort is fabulous," Carrie said. She didn't want him to think she was knocking the place. "Very elegant. We just need to keep building on that foundation." She ticked off several ideas for the future success of the Grand Portofino.

Jack nodded. "You know, everything else aside, I'm glad I followed my gut and hired you for this project."

"Of course you are," Carrie said, her expression flat. "I'm the only PR person you'll ever find who will call you out on your bullshit."

A short burst of laughter escaped Jack's lips. "You're very direct," he said. "Has anyone ever told you?"

Carrie smiled at what she considered a compliment. The reverent look on Jack's face told her it was meant as one. "I've always believed in speaking my mind. My boss wouldn't tolerate me any other way."

They were in front of the Aria Resort & Casino. Jack stopped walking. "Well, I'm going to stop in here and take a look around." He leaned in a little closer. "Care to join me?"

Carrie surveyed the entrance of the hotel. Nothing in the world sounded more appealing than spending more time with Jack Dillon, but she resisted the impulse. "We've made it a whole twenty minutes without arguing," she said, determined to keep the mood light and casual. "That's a record for us. Why push our luck?"

"Oh, come on," he pressed. "I'll buy you a drink."

Jack's face was close to hers now, close enough he could lean in and kiss her if he wanted. And she wanted him to kiss her. Standing there on Las Vegas Boulevard, the buzz of the crowd passing by, the energy of the city throbbing all around them. It was the perfect moment for a kiss.

She traced his chiseled jawline with her gaze, noticing for the first time the texture of the five o'clock shadow that roughened his skin. She couldn't help but remember what it had felt like last night in the elevator. He had devoured her skin with his lips, his rough cheek sparking flames of desire, leaving her body aching and wanting more. She longed to touch his face again, to let her fingers glide over those lips. They had held so much promise the night before. To feel Jack's hands on her body, stirring desires she could not remember ever experiencing before.

Carrie shivered, thinking about the intensity of their encounter and how easily Jack brought her to a mind-boggling climax. It was too easy to imagine what they could have shared if the elevator hadn't snapped back into action. The thought of it sent a tantalizing flurry of tingles shimmying up her spine. But at the same time, it terrified her.

She could deal with Jack on a professional level,

but this overwhelming desire that overcame her every time the two of them were together left her scared to death of losing control.

With a gentle smile, she shook her head and forced her gaze to break away from his. "Jack, I'm glad we ran into each other tonight and had this chance to talk, but I think it would be a good idea for both of us if we limited our time together to strictly business."

"This is business," he said. "I told you, I'm checking on the competition."

Carrie held her ground. "I've already done my rounds for the evening."

"Okay." Jack let it go, and she breathed an inward sigh of relief. The man knew when not to pressure a deal.

"I'm going to catch a cab back to the Grand Portofino," she said.

"Do a little gambling?"

"No, I'm not a big gambler." She shrugged and offered an apologetic smile. "Anyway, I'm here to work, not play."

Jack followed her to the front of the Aria where a short line of people waited for taxis. "I don't gamble, either."

"You own a casino, but you don't gamble?"

"What would be the point?" A playful glint flashed in his warm brown eyes. "Besides, I hate gambling."

"Then why build a casino? Why not something else?" she asked. "A resort in Palm Springs?"

"I already have one of those."

Carrie rocked back on her heels, unable to resist a tease. "So let me get this straight. You don't like to gamble, but you build a casino. Haven't you ever heard of doing something you believe in?"

A taxi pulled forward and Jack opened the door. Only after she had slid into the back seat did he lean forward into the cab and reply, "I'm an investor, Carrie. I believe in making money." He winked as he closed the door.

A flicker of amusement rippled through her. She was baiting him, but he seemed to be enjoying the game just as much as she was. Leaning through the taxi's open window, she mused, "It's too bad a person has to earn a living doing something he doesn't even enjoy."

"You're right," he said, a quirky smile tugging at his lips. "That's why I hired Mark Jergens...the best casino manager in the state of Nevada."

Chapter Five

Mark Jergens was in the casino's surveillance room when Jack returned to the Grand Portofino. Jack found him leaning back in his leather chair, his ankles crossed on the console as he studied the twenty-six monitors which composed the office wall.

Though most people didn't realize it when they entered the casino, cameras were everywhere, and they recorded every move they made. There wasn't a single spot in the Grand Portofino—both on the floor and behind the scenes—that wasn't under surveillance at all times. Each monitor observed a different section of the casino floor. Mark could control each hidden camera, or "eye in the sky" as they were called, from his switchboard-like desk, zooming in on just about anywhere, anyone, anything on the casino floor.

Right now, Mark had a camera focused on the tall brunette seated at one of the dollar slot machines. It captured the lady from the side, but every time she reached to pull the arm of the slot machine, Mark was presented with a great view of her cleavage on the monitor. Jack smirked as he approached unnoticed.

"Pretty girl," he observed. Startled, Mark dropped his feet to the floor and stood to greet him.

"Hey, Jack." Mark turned his attention away from the brunette on the monitor, attempting without success to hide his surprise and embarrassment. He straightened

69

his tie. "I was just doing a quick check of the floor before running downstairs for the midnight pull."

Like most of the major casinos, the Grand Portofino followed a strict schedule of removing cash from the casino floor several times a day. Guards collected the drop boxes from each of the game tables. Both the dealers and pit bosses signed off on the pick-up. Then the cash was transported to the count room, where workers counted and recorded the day's take. The process was swift and discreet for security reasons and to make sure the gambling wasn't interrupted for more than a few moments. In Las Vegas, time was money. Every minute a player wasn't playing, the casino lost money.

"Busy night?" Jack asked, scanning the monitors. The casino was full of people, even more packed than the other hotels on the Strip he'd visited earlier.

"It's hustling all right." Mark nodded in approval. "It'll be even busier on Friday when the weekend crowds come into town."

Jack smiled with satisfaction. Competition was high among the many casinos on the Vegas Strip. All the glitz and glamour in the world didn't mean a thing if a casino wasn't filled with people placing their bets. He had a lot riding on the Grand Portofino's success. It was just one of the reasons he was so keen on getting a new PR firm in place.

But he hadn't stopped by the casino's security office to talk business. Besides being a loyal employee, Mark was one of the few men Jack trusted. They had spent many late nights bullshitting about women in the surveillance room, and sometimes over beers on the Strip, and even once at a strip club on Frank Giotto's birthday. Though Mark was a few years older, both men were single and had a lot in common when it came to work and women. Jack was counting on his friend to help put his priorities back into focus.

It was on the tip of Jack's tongue to tell Mark about his tryst with Carrie when the phone rang. He shifted in his seat as he waited for Mark to finish his call with the casino floor.

"Sorry." Mark placed the phone on the desk. His eyebrows drew together as he finally noticed the uncomfortable expression on Jack's face. "Was there something you needed, boss?"

Boss. Feeling suddenly ridiculous, Jack sighed, finding himself at a loss for words. What was he going to say? *Gee Mark, I have a crush on this witty, funny, gorgeous girl, but she doesn't like me back.* Friend or not, there was no way in hell he'd let that happen.

He scrambled to think of another excuse for stopping into the surveillance room, but before he could speak, Mark exclaimed, "Hey, look, isn't that Carrie Thomas?"

As if the mere thought of her conjured up the actual woman, Jack followed Mark's gaze to one of the security monitors, which overlooked the hotel's main lobby. It was Carrie, all right; Carrie still wearing her little black dress. Only watching her from the camera's overhead viewpoint gave Jack a new perspective on her heavenly figure. Her long legs glided across the marble floor toward the elevator bank, blonde hair bouncing and shining under the lobby's bright lighting.

"Holy cow." Mark shifted in his seat and zoomed in with the camera, checking over his shoulder first to make sure nobody else in the surveillance room was looking except for the two of them.

"She is one hot woman," Mark said, his eagle eyes fixed on the monitor. "Not the uptight business suit she was wearing this morning, huh?"

"Hey, cut it out." Jack peeled his attention away, ashamed for staring so long.

Ignoring him, Mark followed Carrie with the camera, watching until she disappeared into one of the elevators. "She sure is a looker."

"You think so?" Jack said, forcing his voice to sound casual. "I never noticed."

Mark burst out laughing. "Hey, you're talking to me, remember? You spent five hours trapped with her in an elevator wearing nothing but your underwear, and now you're telling me you never noticed she was hot? Give me a freaking break."

"Okay, okay, I noticed." Jack smacked him on the shoulder. "But I'm not paying you to check out women in the casino with my security cameras."

Mark dismissed the reprimand with a wave of his hand, fully aware Jack was trying to change the subject and not buying it for a minute. "Are you ever going to tell me what happened last night, or should I just use my dirty old man imagination?"

Jack coughed and shifted his weight. Mark was an intelligent man. He'd spent thirty years working in the casino business; he knew how to read a cheat like a book. There was no way he'd buy anything Jack had to say unless it was the truth.

"I kissed her, nothing else." Jack opted for the PG-rated version of the story.

Mark nearly fell from his chair. "Jesus, Jack, I was just giving you shit! Are you telling me something *did* happen with her?"

"Yes, but keep your damn mouth shut." Jack sighed. "Carrie made me promise I wouldn't tell anyone."

Despite his instinct to keep his personal life private, Jack told Mark about their tryst last night and his run-in with her at the Bellagio.

"I like her," he confessed. "She's not afraid to speak her mind. And it's nice to talk to a woman I know for sure isn't making a play to see what she can get from me."

Mark was the one guy he trusted. They had talked in the past about women who had clawed their way into his life, simply with the goal of trying to land a rich guy or use his connections to get where they wanted to go. But Carrie was different. There was something about her that humbled him.

"She doesn't want anyone to think I gave her agency the account because of what happened between us." He concluded the story with Carrie's refusal to see him outside of work.

"Beautiful and smart." Mark nodded. "Too bad it probably makes you want her all the more."

"What are you talking about?" Jack's eyebrows shot up. "I don't want her at all. That's what I'm telling you. And even if I did, the last thing I have time for these days is a relationship."

"Okay, boss," Mark said. "You keep telling yourself that."

Jack shot him a resentful glare. What he had said was true. He didn't have time for a relationship. And as enticing as the prospect of being with Carrie was, pursuing her was pointless. For one thing, the demands of opening the Grand Portofino had him stretched to the point of snapping, and if he was going to take the time to get to know a woman, it had to be one with whom he could build a future, not a woman who lived on the opposite end of the country.

Then there were the more practical reasons. Carrie worked for the public relations firm he hired, and dating a client was not a place she was willing to go.

And, of course, the most obvious reason of all. She had already rejected him.

"It's the classic challenge, Jack," Mark said. "Men like to chase what they can't have. Seems to me this one might be worth catching."

"You don't know what you're talking about." Jack stood to leave the surveillance room. He had confided in Mark hoping to forget about Carrie, not to be convinced she was worth going after.

"Oh, I think I do," Mark said. "I might not have a lot of experience with women, but if there's one thing I'm an expert in, it's human behavior."

"I thought you were dating that nurse from Summerlin."

"Sheila?" Mark shook his head. "We've been over for months. She got tired of all the late hours I put in. Where have you been, buddy?"

"Sorry." He shrugged. "I guess I've just been working too hard lately to pay attention to anything else."

"Keep working so much and your entire life will pass you by." The intensity of the look Mark gave Jack matched his rueful words. "Listen to me. If you like this girl, don't let a little challenge get in the way. Sometimes, in the end, you appreciate more the things you have to fight for."

Mark stood. "I've got to run. They're expecting me in the casino."

Jack watched him exit the room, feeling like an ass for not knowing he'd broken up with Sheila, or anything else happening in his life, for that matter. Like him, Mark was married to his work. He knew Mark had tried his hand at relationships when he was younger, but he'd never made them a priority. And now he was alone.

Jack stared at the wall of monitors, weighing his friend's words. It was obvious Mark didn't want him to make the same mistakes he had.

****

The next several days flew by in a blur for Carrie. Her workdays at the Grand Portofino were evolving into a metaphor of Las Vegas itself—a whirlwind of color and food and faces and action. It seemed as if every day she met new people and learned new things about Las Vegas and the casino business.

Even though Jack owned the hotel, Carrie had no idea how many people it took to run the place. There were managers for every department, and each had a huge staff to keep those departments running like clockwork. Entertainment, gaming, housekeeping, conventions, food and beverage, retail, reservations, accounting, marketing, special events—the list went on and on.

And she sat through meetings with every one of them.

Although Jack was occupied with other business, she did see him from time to time. But their meetings were brief and strictly professional.

Which was a good thing, Carrie reminded herself, every single time they interacted.

Though she would die before ever admitting it to him, she was glad to be staying in Las Vegas while she worked on the account. Not only did it allow her the opportunity to better learn the business, but she was also enjoying exploring the city and spending time with the members of Jack's senior staff.

After grueling days of sitting through meetings and working nonstop, it was a good release to hit the town and experience Vegas as a tourist. Other nights, she ordered room service and worked late, or simply took advantage of the peace and quiet of her hotel suite.

Every morning before work, she joined a yoga class at the hotel's fitness center. On the rare afternoon when she could get away, Carrie indulged in a visit to the Grand Portofino's tropical pool area, letting the warm water wash away her stress as she swam under the hot desert sun.

As Carrie emerged from the shower one morning, a knock at the suite door took her by surprise. Rubbing her damp hair with a thick white bath towel, she opened it to find a bellhop holding a large gift-wrapped box.

"Carrie Thomas?"

"Yes?" She pulled the ties of her bathrobe tighter around her waist.

"For you, compliments of Mr. Dillon." The bellhop handed her the box and she stared, caught at a loss for words. By the time she had gathered her wits enough to speak and attempt to offer him a tip, he was halfway down the hall.

Carrie closed the door and walked across the room, shaking her head. She placed the box on her desk and stared at it for a moment, debating whether or not to open it. Morning sunlight poured through the floor-to-ceiling window of her suite, glinting off the shiny silver wrapping paper. She eyed the small envelope tucked under the red satin bow adorning the box.

Dropping her towel on the chair, she gave in and lifted the envelope from under the bow. She opened it, careful not to tear the thick cream-colored stationery.

Even if he hadn't signed the note, she would have known in an instant it was from Jack. The handwriting was neat, sharp, and dark as if he had pressed the pen extra hard into the Grand Portofino notecard it was written on, with a quick, commanding signature at the end. It all but screamed power and self-assurance. Just like the man.

She smiled and read the note.

Carrie,

I'll try not to get this one jammed in the door. Dinner tonight at Steak House, seven o'clock. I've missed you.

Jack

She slid the red bow off the box and lifted the lid. She knew what it was even before she finished removing the layers of tissue paper. She lifted the Louis Vuitton Monogram tote out of the box and gasped at its exquisiteness.

She had never owned a Louis Vuitton before, and this one was amazing. It had a splash of pink on its interior lining to complement the famous brown monogrammed design on the outside. Almost the same shade of pink as her old bag, the one damaged in the revolving glass door incident.

Carrie swept a tendril of damp hair away from her

face and admired the new bag. Ever since her first impression of Jack, she was forever revising her opinion of him. It wasn't the price tag but the thoughtfulness of this amazing gift that sent her heart soaring and made her like him even more.

Her pulse quickened, and she wondered if he had chosen it himself. She suspected he had; it was perfect. She could almost picture him wandering around the Louis Vuitton boutique at the Grand Portofino's concourse shops until he saw this bag and knew it was the one. The idea that he knew her so well sent delicious tremors of happiness tingling through her body.

She wished he had delivered the gift in person. Carrie grabbed the phone on her desk and dialed the extension to Jack's office.

"Mr. Dillon is in a meeting right now," Grace, his assistant, announced airily after Carrie asked to speak with him. "Do you care to leave a message?"

The flicker of disappointment came as a surprise. She hadn't realized how much she'd been looking forward to talking to Jack until Grace told her he was not there.

"Please tell him I said thank you." She fiddled with the red bow, trying to keep the chagrin from creeping into her voice. "He'll know what it's regarding."

With the excitement of the morning behind her, Carrie settled into her workday. She got dressed and returned to her desk in the living room of her suite, but the red-ribboned box kept stealing her attention from the pile of work she needed to do. She forced herself to concentrate on the press release she was writing, but it was no use.

She rose and crossed the room to the elegant yellow armchair where she had placed the box. She reread Jack's note with a hardened eye.

His invitation to dinner was an innocent request, but for some reason, the words sent her guard flying straight up. It was hard enough getting through each day without thoughts of him distracting her. How was she supposed to sit through dinner with this man?

She had to remember her whole career teetered on the success of this press event she was organizing. Carrie thought she had made it pretty clear to him their relationship was to remain strictly business, but it sounded like he was planning a romantic evening for two.

Or was she just jumping to conclusions? She sank back into the armchair and read the note again. It wasn't unusual for a client to take her to dinner. It happened all the time in New York. But of course, in New York, her clients weren't men she had almost gone down on in a stalled elevator.

She sighed and returned to her desk. Working for Jack Dillon would be much easier if she wasn't so damned attracted to him. And she was there to work, not play, right? Then why was the notion of spending a romantic evening alone with him far more appealing than spending the evening working on his PR campaign?

She'd have to decline his invitation; there was no other option. After their team meeting this afternoon, she'd let him know she had too much work to do to go to dinner. And it wasn't a lie. The opening of Cardini's was less than two weeks away, and she hadn't even finished writing the press release yet.

Get your shit together, Carolyn Thomas. She berated herself. *You've got a lot of work to do.*

****

Rejecting Jack's invitation, however, was much easier said than done.

The afternoon team meeting took place inside the new restaurant, instead of the usual conference room on the thirtieth floor. All the hotel's top leaders were present when Carrie arrived, but Jack was nowhere in sight.

Although the grand opening was still a few weeks off, the interior designers had already put most of the final touches on the restaurant. Like Antonio Cardini's other establishments, it was tastefully decorated with dim lighting and rich leather booths, featuring a meandering layout instead of one open room, creating lots of cozy corners perfect for intimate conversation.

Carrie took her seat at the table and focused on the work at hand. She was scheduled to present her strategy for the restaurant's grand opening press event. She had poured her heart and soul into developing this communications plan, and right now her sole focus was to get everyone's buy-in.

By the time Jack arrived, the meeting had already begun, and she was deep into her presentation. From the corner of her eye, she watched him take a chair next to her but dared not look his way as she continued speaking to the group. No matter what was swirling through her mind and in her heart, Carrie was resolved to maintain a professional air around Jack and his staff.

"Antonio will be here on Monday," she said. "And he's ready to rock and roll. He's been in constant contact with his team, overseeing all the details of the new restaurant. I've asked him to have the menu for Saturday night's event finalized so we can print menu cards. I want all the journalists who attend the event to have a take-away for reference."

"Who's coming?" Jack broke in. He leaned back in his chair, twisting the cap off one of the bottles of water Grace had set out for the meeting.

She turned in his direction. An unexpected jolt of electricity rocketed across her skin as her leg accidentally brushed his under the table. At her touch, Jack bolted upright and pulled away, but not before Carrie, too, shifted her position, crossing her legs the other way. They both scrambled to reposition, and they touched again.

Carrie uncrossed her legs and pushed her seat back a few inches to create more space between them. They exchanged awkward, apologetic smiles.

So much for cool and professional. She hoped the heat creeping up her cheeks was not evident.

She responded to his question. "So far I've got commitments from two major local newspapers. I think several Las Vegas tourist websites and TV stations will send reporters over, too. Not to mention a pretty impressive guest list Antonio has prepared. He has a lot of connections in Los Angeles."

Jack took a long sip of water, then picked up one of the press releases from the table. He scanned it and nodded his approval.

"After you've approved the releases, we can have them printed and send out press kits," Carrie said. "As long as we overnight them by tomorrow, we'll have enough lead time to get the national food and travel magazines who can't attend. And we'll get the digital materials posted on the Grand Portofino's website. I think we're going to have a pretty strong response."

She turned to Jack. "I've already interviewed Antonio for his bio. It would be great if you have time this afternoon to go over yours."

"We can talk about it over dinner tonight," he said.

Carrie froze for the briefest moment, surprised he had referenced his dinner invitation in front of the entire group. A devilish glint sparkled in the depths of his dark eyes as her gaze locked onto his—as if daring her to argue—but it was impossible to say a word about it with everyone watching.

"Fine," she said, all business.

Forty minutes later, the meeting ended with an extensive to-do list jotted in her planner. As the room emptied, she took her time gathering the papers spread across the table. She was acutely aware of Jack standing behind her chair, waiting, and she wanted to make sure they were alone before she turned to face him and say what needed to be said.

"This is a great bag." At last, she stood, packing the last of her belongings into the new Louis Vuitton. Unwelcome pangs fluttered through her stomach like frayed wires short-circuiting. "Thank you so much."

"You're welcome." Jack held the door for her as they exited the restaurant. "Heading upstairs? I'll walk to the elevators with you."

"You know," Carrie said, her voice tentative. They fell into stride. "It's been a few days since I heard from you. I wasn't sure if I'd see you again at all."

"I wasn't sure if you wanted to hear from me," Jack admitted. "But as you can see, I decided to take a chance."

Walking across the casino floor, they were besieged by a symphony of clanging slot machines and the electrifying beat of music playing over the sound system. Even in the afternoon, the casino buzzed with people hoping to win big. Jack surveyed the sight with a look of satisfaction on his face.

"The casino's doing well." Carrie followed his gaze across the sprawling casino floor. "You must be pleased."

"All casinos do well," he said. "With an investment as big as this one, failure isn't an option."

"I get the feeling 'failure isn't an option' is your motto with everything in life." She tossed him one of her teasing grins. Somehow, Carrie just knew Jack was the kind of man who always got what he wanted.

They walked together in silence through the maze of the casino. After a few minutes, Jack raised an eyebrow in her direction. It was clear he sensed something was on her mind, and from the pensive expression on his face, knew it wasn't good.

Carrie took a deep breath. "About dinner tonight…"

"Seven o'clock okay with you?"

Damn, he wasn't making this easy. Her excuse of having too much work to do suddenly seemed transparent as a sheet of glass. "Jack," she said, "I don't think it's a good idea for you and me to see each other outside of work."

"It's just dinner, Carrie," he said. "I'm a busy person and you're a busy person, so let's call this an opportunity to talk business and get to know each other a little better. I mean, we have to eat, right?"

Jack's logic frustrated the hell out of her. How

could she argue? She stepped aside to let a scantily clad cocktail waitress carrying a full tray of drinks move past them. They paused, standing next to a row of slot machines. A tendril of cigarette smoke from a nearby player drifted past. Carrie detested the smell of cigarettes, but she ignored the acrid scent as it wafted over them and held his gaze.

"Look," she began, taking a deep breath she hoped Jack wouldn't notice, "it's pretty obvious something is hanging between us, but I'm not about to let a little chemistry get in the way of my career. You're my client, and I have a job to do, deadlines to meet, and I don't think we should confuse things by getting involved."

There. She'd said it. Carrie was not usually one to hesitate when she had something important to say, but every time she talked to Jack, her entire brain shifted off-kilter. She was relieved to have spoken her mind.

"Carrie..." Jack reached for her hand, but she pulled it away. "I don't bite."

She exhaled a deep sigh. "I'm sorry." For a long moment, she stood with her gaze locked on his, lost in her uneasiness and the sea of people drifting through the casino. Why was just being alone with him always such an effort? If she didn't want to hit him, she wanted to kiss him, and neither option would prove very conducive to their working relationship.

Jack's brow creased. "Let me ask you a question. If we were in New York and I was a random married old client suggesting we go to dinner to discuss business, would you turn me down?"

"Come on, Jack." Carrie struggled to maintain control of the situation. "You can't ignore what happened between us."

"Look," he said, "I respect how dedicated you are to your career, and I am sure you'll do a great job for my hotel. I just want to get to know you a little better, as a colleague. Is that so wrong?"

She studied the pattern on the casino's carpeting. Maybe he was right. Maybe she was overthinking it. Was it really any different from the night before, when she went to dinner with Sherry and Mark?

Of course, it was different, Carrie reminded herself. Mark Jergens hadn't made her come on the floor of an elevator.

"Okay, I have an idea." Sensing her unwavering hesitancy, Jack pulled a bill from his wallet and held it for Carrie to observe. "You need to interview me for this bio you want to write, and I want to take you to dinner."

He approached the slot machine they were standing in front of and motioned toward it. "Let's leave it to fate. If this machine hits, I take you to dinner tonight, and we do the interview there. If it doesn't, we'll do the interview tomorrow in the office, and I'll never bother you again. Deal?"

Carrie's gaze swept over him. "I thought you didn't gamble."

"You're worth the risk," he said, inserting the twenty into the slot machine. The machine sucked it in. "Besides, the odds are in your favor. Go ahead."

"You want me to do it?"

"Sure, why not?" He stepped aside, his smile unraveling her.

Carrie approached the slot machine. "If this machine loses, you'll leave me alone?"

"Absolutely." With crossed arms and an infuriating smirk, Jack leaned against the neighboring slot machine. She reached forward to press the machine's Spin button, but he seized her hand, stopping her. "No, pull the arm. More fun than pressing a button."

Carrie raised an eyebrow but pulled the slot machine's arm. Her heartbeat quickened as the machine sprang to life. She watched with drawn breath as the reels spun in a blazing stream of color.

The first one stopped on a gold seven. The second one stopped on a gold seven. Her eyes widened with anticipation. When the third reel stopped to reveal three gold sevens in a row, a bell rang, and wild music began playing from the slot machine.

Without thinking, she let out a whoop and threw her arms around Jack's neck. She barely heard his hearty "Congratulations" over the symphony of sounds.

Then, realizing she had actually *lost* the bet, Carrie pounded her fist against his rock-hard chest. "Damn you, Jack. You had this planned all along."

He raised his hands in defense. "I did not. Face it, Carrie, you've got the magic touch."

As their winnings multiplied on the machine's little digital screen, Jack advised, "Might want to use that cash to buy yourself something nice to wear tonight. I'll pick you up at seven?"

"I'll meet you there," she conceded.

Jack's smile widened in approval. He took a step backward. "See you later," he called over the clang of the machine, turning to leave her alone with their winnings.

Carrie couldn't help but laugh at the irony as she watched first Jack's retreat, and then the winning dollar amount on the slot machine continue to increase. Leave it to her to have beginner's luck and hit the jackpot, the one time in her life she was betting to lose.

But she wasn't disappointed. No, she was happy. In fact, she couldn't remember the last time she felt this full of joy. And—she shuddered at the realization—her exultation had nothing to do with the winnings she was about to cash in.

Chapter Six

Jack was already seated when Carrie arrived at Steak House. As a hostess escorted her across the restaurant to their table, he rose to greet her. She was taken aback, as always, by his striking appearance. Though tonight, instead of the usual tailored suit she had expected to find him in, he was wearing dark jeans, a black button-down shirt, and a black blazer.

She sucked in her breath at the tantalizing sight. *Holy crap.*

He dropped a casual kiss on her cheek and pulled out a chair. "You look beautiful."

"Thank you." Carrie eased into her seat. She had debated wearing business attire herself for their dinner meeting, but instead opted for a deep blue dress that showed off her tan with its elegant, silky halter top, and she was grateful for her decision. She had swept her hair into a loose bun, and wispy strands fell around her face, brushing against the dangling earrings she had purchased on her shopping spree. She pushed a strand of hair off her cheek and smiled at him.

Jack nodded at the waiter, who retrieved a bottle of wine from the ice bucket beside their table and poured Carrie a glass.

"I took the liberty of ordering already," he said. "Hope you don't mind."

Carrie smiled, forcing herself to be gracious. Under

normal circumstances, she loathed when a man made decisions for her. But in this fancy restaurant with this high-class man, the gesture seemed appropriate.

Besides, Carrie reminded herself, for the hundredth time. He was a client. And as far as she was concerned, this was a business dinner.

Jack raised his glass. "To fate."

"Fate?" She clinked her glass to his and took a sip of the chilled white wine but couldn't help question his choice of toasts.

"Without fate, we wouldn't be here together tonight."

"Fate and a twenty-dollar bill," Carrie chided.

"Always so cynical." Jack shook his head. "Why?"

"You have to admit, that slot machine hitting the jackpot was a pretty big coincidence." She took another sip of wine.

"So you don't believe fate had a hand in any of this?" he challenged. "That maybe you stepping on the elevator and us getting stuck together, and then hitting the jackpot on a one-in-a-million chance means maybe there's some higher force bringing us together?"

Jack never ceased to amaze her. "You talk like such a romantic for a serious businessman."

"I *am* a romantic," he said, setting his wineglass on the table and piercing her with his gaze. "And you're avoiding the question. Do you really think us getting stuck together, not once but twice in the same day, is pure coincidence? What if I had stepped into a different elevator or been stopped by a stranger and asked the time and been three seconds later stepping into the revolving glass door?"

"Or if my plane hadn't been delayed, I would have

arrived in Vegas an hour earlier, and we would have never gotten stuck together at all."

"So you do see what I'm getting at."

Carrie studied her wineglass, contemplating how much she wanted to share. The years she had spent building her professional image had honed a cool exterior. But something about Jack tonight made her walls start to crumble, despite the pep talks she'd given herself and promises to keep her guard up.

"Okay, I'll tell you something." At last she gave in. "But you have to promise not to laugh."

"I promise." Jack leaned back in his chair. The restaurant was dark, and the soft candlelight flickering on the table between them reflected in his eyes and cast long shadows across his clean-shaven face.

"I have this thing I call my Laundry Room Philosophy."

A burst of laugher cut her off, and Carrie's mouth set in annoyance. "Never mind."

"I'm sorry." Jack collected himself right away. "You just surprised me."

"Do you want to hear it or not?"

He leaned forward and touched her hand on the table, apologizing again. "Yeah, I do. Go ahead."

Carrie hesitated for a moment before continuing. "Five years ago, I was working at a tiny PR agency as a receptionist, living in this old building in Greenwich Village. I hated my job, hated my roommate, having a real hard time with money, and thinking about moving back home with my parents."

Jack nodded with understanding, and Carrie continued. "So one Saturday morning in the middle of all this turmoil, I go to the laundry room in my building and there, folding her clothes, was a woman I had never seen before. We get to talking. Turns out she lives in the penthouse of my building and is a partner at this successful PR agency. Tells me they are looking for a new assistant account executive and asks if I want to interview."

"Phyllis Dailey," he interjected.

"Yes." Carrie raised her glass to her lips and swallowed the last sip of wine. Was her story that predictable, or was Jack just that perceptive? "That's how I met Phyllis."

Jack refilled her wineglass as she continued. "So I meet Phyllis, get a higher-paying job, move into a nicer apartment, work my way up in the company, fly to Las Vegas on business, get *held hostage*—" She flashed a teasing smile. "—and now here we are having dinner together."

"And you don't call that fate?"

"No." Carrie shook her head. "Simply events leading to events leading to still other events leading to this one chance moment in time when you and I are here having dinner together tonight."

"So what you're saying is, if you hadn't been doing laundry in that exact place at that exact moment five years ago, we wouldn't be sitting together here in this restaurant right now."

"Exactly." She tossed him a triumphant smile. She didn't know if it was the wine, or the candlelight, or the relaxed banter between them, but she found herself colossally glad she'd been doing laundry that day.

The waiter arrived with an appetizer and set their plates on the table.

"What's this?" Carrie welcomed the opportunity to

change the subject.

"Artichoke dip and breadsticks." Jack picked up a breadstick and swiped it through the bowl of dip at the center of the plate. The creamy dip oozed down the side of the breadstick as he raised it toward his mouth.

Seeing Carrie's inquisitive expression, he asked, "Don't you like artichoke dip?"

"I've never tried it," she admitted. "Artichokes are not very big on the East Coast."

"Oh, yes," he said. "I keep forgetting I'm dealing with a New Yorker. Allow me to introduce you."

He slid his chair closer and reached to dip a fresh breadstick into the artichoke dip. Steam rose from the bowl, swirling around Jack's strong, big hand.

Carrie took one, too, but before she could bring it to her mouth, Jack's hand was there, offering her a bite of his. He leaned in close, so close the fresh scent of his soap tickled her senses. The fresh, masculine scent brought memories of their night trapped together on the elevator hurtling into her consciousness.

She met his gaze and opened her mouth, obeying his wordless request, and Jack slid the breadstick between her lips. She bit down slowly, her teeth sinking into the soft dough. Warm, white, creamy dip dripped down the side of the breadstick.

Without releasing his gaze, her tongue emerged to lick it away, swiping his finger with it in the process. "Yummy."

Jack's lip upturned in the tiniest tick of a smirk. He wriggled in his seat, adjusting his jeans ever so slightly, and Carrie felt victorious. She reached for one of the carrot sticks garnishing their appetizer.

"Now you try this," she instructed, her voice heavy

and seductive. She dipped it into the artichoke dip and held it to his lips. Now his smirk curled into a full, heated smile. She slipped the carrot stick into his mouth.

Her fingers lingered on his lips as he chewed and swallowed. Jack took advantage, kissing the tips of her manicured fingertips. Then he traced her fingers with his tongue, slipped one into his mouth, and bit down gently, sucking and kissing it. Carrie let her eyes drop closed, and her body throbbed in response.

They were playing with fire, and she knew it. But she was lost in the erotic moment, and even if she wanted to pull her fingers away, she didn't think she could. At last, Jack released her. He turned his head, pressing his cheek to hers, his lips brushing her neck and ear as her fingers trembled against his jaw.

"Do you still think of this as a business dinner?" he whispered, his breath hot against her ear.

Carrie's body went rigid, and her eyes snapped open. Jack's calculated words brought her crashing back to where they were, what they were doing, and how many people were in the room to witness it. She couldn't believe she'd lost control.

The waiter approached their table, saving her from the humiliation of having to respond. He set the plates with their main course on the table.

"Excuse me." She pushed her chair back and stood, so abruptly it almost toppled over. A trip to the ladies' room was without a doubt in order. With cheeks burning, she made her way across the restaurant. *What the hell just happened?*

When she returned to the table, Jack had returned the chairs to their original positions. The artichoke dip was gone, all evidence of what transpired between them wiped away. He even stood to greet her, a formal gesture considering he had her fingers in his mouth just a few minutes before.

"Are you okay?" he asked, taking his seat again.

"I'm great." Carrie nodded and flashed him her best high-watt smile. She had pressed the reset button on her brain in the bathroom, forcing the cool and professional version of herself to hop back into the driver's seat. But under the facade, she was mad as hell for letting her attraction to Jack make her forget why she was there. She couldn't let it happen again. The idea of getting caught with Jack in a compromising position made her shudder.

She studied her dinner plate, the forced smile still glued to her face as she took in the artfully arranged surf and turf.

"Don't you like lobster?"

"Huh?" Carrie's attention snapped his way. Jack was studying her with concern.

"You're staring at your plate with a funny look on your face," he said. "Don't tell me you've never had lobster before, either."

She smoothed the linen napkin on her lap. Her guilty shrug was enough of a confession.

If Jack was surprised, he failed to show it. "Let me help you." He demonstrated how to break off the meat. Instead of feeding her this time, he handed her a forkful.

Carrie took her first bite. "It's good," she said, but the foreign flavor on her tongue was still too new to judge.

Jack couldn't have looked more pleased if he had

boiled that bad boy himself. With a satisfied smile, he began to help Carrie with her next bite, but she pulled away.

"I don't need you to cut my meat for me. I'm not a child." Who did he think he was...her ex-fiancé? David was notorious for treating her like she couldn't even get through a meal without him mansplaining how to do it.

The injured look in his eyes was unmistakable. "I didn't think I was treating you like a child."

Carrie swallowed her bite of lobster and sighed. No doubt she was being unreasonable, but the artichoke dip situation had left her on edge. Who knew an appetizer could be so damn seductive? "I'm sorry. I only meant I can do it myself."

He gestured toward her plate as if to say, "go ahead." She surveyed the food and reached down to break off a piece of meat from one of the lobster claws.

Jack jumped in, his voice laced with urgency. "I wouldn't do—" But the icy look Carrie shot silenced him. She was resolved to do it on her own.

The lobster claw snapped off with such force, it went sailing through the air and landed in the intricate hairdo of an older woman sitting at the next table over. Engaged in animated conversation, neither the woman nor her companion noticed the bright red chunk of lobster protruding obtrusively from the back of her white-blonde upsweep. They continued to talk, the claw sticking out as the woman's head bobbed.

Carrie's hand flew over her mouth as she gasped in disbelief. Following her horrified gaze, Jack turned in his seat just in time to see the waiter serving the couple's dinner. The woman tilted her head to thank him, but the lobster claw in her hairdo remained intact.

There was no doubt it was there to stay.

He nearly choked, struggling to suppress his laughter. He gulped the rest of his wine to hide his reaction.

"What should we do?" Carrie gushed, her voice a panicked whisper. Never before had she been faced with such a dilemma. "I'm going to tell her."

She placed her napkin on the table and stood, her intentions clear, but Jack caught her wrist and pulled her down into the chair. "No, you'll embarrass her."

"But we can't just—" Watching the woman eat her dinner with the big red lobster claw in her near-white hair was too much. She leaned forward in her chair, laughter threatening to roll from her lips.

Jack stole another look behind him. Biting his cheek, he asked, "Want to get out of here?"

She nodded, the linen napkin pressed against her lips to hide the broad grin threatening to erupt into laughter at any moment. He rose and took her hand in his, leading her across the restaurant so fast she had to run to keep up with his long strides.

Still holding her hand, Jack stopped at the reservation stand and pointed to the couple they just dodged.

"May I help you, Mr. Dillon?" the hostess asked.

"Please make sure those people are taken care of. I want their entire meal to be comped."

"Of course, sir," she obliged, jotting a note. "Shall I give them a reason?"

"They'll figure it out."

Outside the restaurant, Carrie took one look at Jack and they both exploded in laughter, clinging to each other for balance as their bodies shook. Like two misbehaving teenagers, they laughed uncontrollably, oblivious to the spectacle they made of themselves to curious passers-by.

"Did you see…" But Jack couldn't even finish his sentence before a fresh round of laughter roared out of him. He grasped her shoulder for support.

Carrie wiped the tears from her cheeks and attempted to catch her breath. "Oh my God, I can't remember when I ever laughed so hard in my life." Even as she spoke, her words danced with more giggles.

"I'll never be able to eat lobster again," he said. "The image of that poor lady with a lobster claw in her hair is etched into my mind forever."

"Me too."

Jack shook his finger at her. "And why the hell do you always have to be so damn stubborn?"

She shrugged at his question, guilty, but not willing to admit it.

He sighed when their laughter finally subsided. "Still hungry?"

"Ravenous."

"Where do you want to go? I know this great little French restaurant—"

Carrie cut in, her voice composed and confident. "How about I buy you dinner?"

****

Jack examined the contents of his cardboard tray, his expression wrinkled with both amusement and confusion. "You call this dinner?"

Carrie took a bite of her hot dog, and a glob of sauerkraut and mustard fell from her mouth. With a lighthearted chuckle, she wiped her face with a paper napkin.

"Carolyn Thomas, you never cease to amaze me."

Funny, she had just thought the same thing about him not an hour before.

They stood in front of Nathan's at the New York-New York Hotel & Casino. The Coney Island-themed area was as loud as it was crowded, with young kids buzzing toward the arcade and herds of tourists taking a break from the casino to ride the hotel's famous roller coaster. She was over-dressed in her blue halter dress but so much more comfortable here than she'd been sitting at their table at Steak House.

It had been her idea to cross the street to the nearby hotel, craving something simple to counterbalance the posh ambiance of the restaurant at the Grand Portofino. "I've got simple tastes," she informed Jack, taking a second bite of her hot dog.

"I have no problem enjoying the simple things in life." As if to prove his point, he snatched away one of her chili fries and popped it into his mouth.

They strolled through the arcade, enjoying their hot dogs and watching the people around them. On a dare, Jack challenged her to a game of pinball, which she won, much to his chagrin. Carrie loved a good challenge, and they followed pinball with a stream of other classic arcade games until they were out of tokens and laughing so hard she couldn't remember the last time she had so much fun.

It was late in the evening when they left the arcade and slipped into the piano bar at the New York-New York Casino. The dueling pianos drew a fun audience, and though the place was crowded, they still managed to find two seats at the bar.

Jack ordered a whiskey sour and asked Carrie what she wanted.

"Just a water for me, please. My head is still fuzzy from all the wine we drank earlier." She had to shout to be heard above the energetic buzz of the crowd.

As Jack paid the bartender, she surveyed the lively scene around them. People were jammed everywhere, talking, drinking, and singing along with the pianos.

Following her roving gaze, he said, "See, it's just like being in New York City, so you can't be mad at me anymore for making you stay in Vegas. I'll even hire somebody to mug you if it makes you feel more at home."

"Very funny." Carrie defended her hometown. "New York isn't so bad."

"Oh come on, you can't tell me you're not just a little relieved to be away from the city. I saw you by the pool earlier," he said. "This place is paradise compared to Manhattan."

"You saw me by the pool?" She raised an eyebrow. Needing a break from work, she had slipped on a new white one-piece swimsuit and spent an hour reading an e-book on her phone while lounging outside in the resort's lushly landscaped pool area. Bottled water in hand, eyes shaded against the desert sun, she had no idea anyone had seen her go outside.

"I see you everywhere."

Carrie blinked at the revelation. It stirred her to the core to know he had been watching her, but she'd never give him the satisfaction of admitting it. Ignoring his last comment, she addressed the first part of what he had said. "I can see why Las Vegas attracts so many tourists. But I still could never imagine why anyone would choose to live here."

"It's the fastest growing city in the nation," Jack pointed out. "You'd be surprised at how different it is once you get off the Strip. Maybe one day you'll let me show you."

She gave him a noncommittal nod, and the conversation shifted to other things. They talked with the familiarity of two old friends, comparing their childhoods in different parts of the country, exchanging college stories, high school pranks, and tales of disastrous blind dates.

She laughed at his stories and then listened with interest as he talked about more serious things. He told her how he got involved with real estate, closing his first deal at the age of twenty-four in a small town in Ohio. She couldn't suppress her smile as he spoke, surprised by how much she enjoyed listening to Jack describe his rise in the business world. Never once did she feel like he was being self-centered or dominating the conversation.

Hearing him talk about his life was like getting reacquainted with an old friend. He was no longer just a man she was attracted to—Jack Dillon, owner of the Grand Portofino Resort & Casino, and her client. He was a man she was more comfortable with after a few hours than she had been after years with her ex-fiancé. She could be herself and laugh and talk about her career without shame or belittlement. Getting to know him was the most fun she'd had in ages, and she looked forward to knowing him even better. The prospect excited her.

And scared her to death.

She had to remember why she was there, but she

was having a hard time keeping her priorities in check. She sat rapt as he spoke, studying his handsome, animated face. Mesmerized by his voice and the way the laugh lines around his warm brown eyes deepened when he smiled.

All the while, pianos played and the crowd sang along, creating an electric energy in the bar. But as lit as it was, the excitement of their surroundings paled in comparison to the sparks crackling between them, like Fourth of July fireworks about to go off.

She stared at Jack's face but found his words skipping over her as she became more and more aware of his scent and his breath against her skin. He leaned in, and Carrie realized he was asking her a question.

"Huh?" She tilted her head toward his, caught.

Jack's voice dropped to a husky tone. "I said, don't you wonder what might have happened between us if we met at a different time and place?" His hand came to rest on her knee, sending a hot tingle up her spine.

Carrie nodded, her gaze riveted to his face. She would have said yes if he asked her to jump off the Manhattan Bridge. Jack's voice made her far more intoxicated than even the wine.

"I can hardly think of anything but," she admitted, her voice raspy.

Jack kissed her. It was a quick, impulsive kiss, as if testing the waters to gage her reaction. But when he went to pull away, she pressed her mouth to his and deepened the kiss.

If Jack was surprised, he didn't show it. He slid his hands from her knee up her bare arms, drawing her body nearer, and she responded by parting her lips. His embrace was like a warm summer night, calm and sweet but sprinkled with shooting stars. She melted in his arms.

It was not the fevered passion they had shared in the elevator but a calmer, deeper sensation that made Carrie abandon all other senses and get lost in the moment.

Somewhere in the background, she heard the clamor of the dueling pianos. The two singers led the crowd through a rowdy rendition of a Garth Brooks classic. But as she got lost in the heat of Jack's embrace, the music drifted away as if through a filter, and the voices around them faded from the room.

But then, reason plowed into her like an out-of-control truck, and she pulled back. Jack's hands still grasped her shoulders, but when he opened his eyes and saw the expression on her face, he loosened his grip.

"Carrie, what's wrong?"

"I shouldn't have let this happen." Her voice broke, and she shook her head. His kiss was still hot on her lips.

"Why not?" he demanded, reaching for her hand. "What's so wrong with what we're doing?"

She stared at their entwined fingers. How could she explain to Jack her career was the most important thing in her life? That when relationships failed her, when her parents disappointed her, it was always her work that kept her going? She wanted him. Carrie couldn't deny it anymore. But she had worked too hard for too long to risk losing it all.

"I can't mess around with a client." Her words were firm and final.

"Maybe I don't want to just mess around," he said, his voice equally decisive. "Maybe I want more."

"But Jack," Carrie stammered, her eyes wide at his blunt admission, "we come from opposite ends of the country. And in two weeks I need to go back to mine. My life is in New York and your life is here; there's no way anything more could ever work."

Jack leaned in closer so he wouldn't have to shout above the music. "Don't you think I realize that?" He squeezed her hand in his. "But it's just geography. We could figure something out if we wanted to."

"There's more." She took a deep breath. "My boss is very old-fashioned. My career would be toast if he ever discovered I was dating a client."

"You mean Phyllis?"

"No, of course not Phyllis," Carrie said. "Phyllis is a friend. I think she'd understand. I am talking about Jim Cresswell, the big boss. Owner of the company. He's semi-retired, and I don't see him much, but somehow, he always knows what's going on with who and where. Always."

"Carrie." Jack stared at her in disbelief. "Las Vegas is more than two thousand miles away from New York City."

"No." She shook her head, even before he had finished his sentence. "It's not worth the risk. I know you think I'm being paranoid, but I have a real shot at becoming a senior partner at the agency. How can I risk throwing it all away?"

"I understand." He rubbed his neck. "So we can't get together because if your boss finds out you're dating a client, you won't get the promotion. I can fire your agency, and then I won't be a client…but then you won't get the promotion because you lost the account. It's a no-win situation, and I must say, Carrie," he added, "this Jim Cresswell sounds like a real asshole."

She couldn't suppress her smile. "Yes, but an asshole who signs my paychecks."

"There's more to life than paychecks," he said. Then, with a defeated sigh, added, "I'm not used to having problems I can't solve."

Carrie understood his frustration. Jack was a man accustomed to fixing problems with the snap of his fingers. He had an army of employees, all willing to jump through hoops to give the boss what he wanted. But this one was beyond them both.

"You can't deny something is happening between us."

She shook her head. "No, Jack, I guess I can't. Not anymore."

"So what should we do about it?"

"I don't know," she answered, a dubious mix of craving and confusion blurring her thoughts. "Since the day we met, I've been trying so hard to push you away and pretend like nothing happened between us."

She fought the urge to bury her head against his shoulder, knowing she had to be truthful right now or else it would eat away at her forever. "I can't stop thinking about the way you touched me, and how incredible it felt to kiss you, and what sex might have been like if the elevator hadn't started when it did. I've been trying to forget about you and get on with my job. But here's the truth." She paused and met his eager gaze with hungry eyes. "Every minute I'm with you, I want you more and more."

Jack let out a long, slow breath. "I'm so fucking glad to hear you say that. I feel the same way."

Carrie exhaled, too, feeling one weight lift from

her shoulders at the same moment another crashed down. She was too far gone to turn back now. And if she was being honest with herself, turning back now was the last thing she wanted to do.

"If we don't give in to it, it'll just keep hanging there." She slid her hand seductively under the collar of his shirt. She could feel the heat of his skin and pulse throbbing against her fingertips. "Tempting us."

"Spend the night with me." Jack's voice simmered with a savage desire. "Spend the night with me, Carrie, and I promise it will be one we'll never forget."

She allowed the fantasy to play in her mind. A few days ago, such an offer would have warranted him a slap in the face, but now the proposition enticed her. Didn't she deserve a little excitement in her life? She'd never been one to give in to lust, but she couldn't deny it. The idea of sleeping with Jack was a tempting one. He was her ideal of a man; handsome, classy, funny, brilliant, and sexy as hell. And after their night on the elevator, Carrie just knew making love to him would be like nothing she had ever experienced before.

She'd spent her whole life trying to please other people. Her boss, her parents, even David. Now she wanted something for herself. She was in Las Vegas, after all—Sin City—wasn't she entitled to a little sinning of her own?

"We have two weeks before I return to New York," she countered, feeling deliciously uninhibited. She trailed a finger along his collar. "Why not make the most of what time we do have and not think about what we don't?"

"Two weeks, huh?" There was a bold glint in his dark eyes. "We could have a lot of fun in two weeks."

"Just promise me we'll be discreet." She pressed a finger to his lips. "Nobody else can know."

He kissed her fingertip. "Boy Scout's honor."

Carrie smirked because of course this clean-cut, well-mannered, brilliant man from Ohio had been a Boy Scout. She leaned in to kiss him, but as their lips brushed, Jack pulled back and looked into her eyes.

"Carrie, I have to say this." His voice was solemn. "Before we do anything. I know the only reason you're still here in Las Vegas is because I forced you to stay. That was unfair. If you want to go back to New York, you can. It won't affect the account at all. I want you to be here because you want to be, not because you have to be."

She looked past Jack at the crowd gathered around the dueling pianos. Everyone was smiling and drinking and singing and swaying along to the raucous tune. He had just handed her a ticket home to New York, but the notion was now unappealing. Las Vegas was turning out to be more fun than she'd ever expected, and she wanted to experience everything it had to offer.

Most of all, she wanted to experience those things with him. More than business was riding on how she decided to respond to his offer, and she didn't need to think long.

"I want to stay."

Jack's jaw set in triumph. He slipped an arm around her waist and pulled her close, pressing his whiskey-flavored lips to hers.

This time, the kiss held a promise. And even if they could only promise each other two weeks, it was a gamble Carrie was willing to take.

Chapter Seven

They rode the elevator to her floor in an unexpected uncomfortable silence. At least, for Carrie it was uncomfortable; she suspected Jack's silence was intentional. She had a vision of him pushing her against the wall of the elevator the moment they were alone, smashing his mouth to hers, her knee rising to his hip as their desperate bodies writhed together. But instead of unhinged passion, he stood on the opposite side, gaze fixed on the numbers as they climbed to the eighteenth floor of the Grand Portofino. She wrung her hands together. Was this elevator moving slower than usual?

The endless silence stretched on as they walked down the long hallway to her suite. Jack allowed her to lead the way. Once inside, he hung the Do Not Disturb sign on the handle outside the door, then clicked it shut. He turned and walked across the room to where she stood. Carrie swallowed hard.

Holding her gaze, he switched off the desk lamp. The only light in the room drifted in through the window, an uneasy mix of soft yellow moonlight and the brash neon lights of the Strip below. He touched a button on the wall, and the heavy drapes drew together, the mechanical whir of the cords breaking the silence.

"No, leave them open," she requested. "I like the lights."

Jack smiled and pressed the button again, stopping

the drapes while they were still a few feet apart.

At last, he spoke. "Music?"

She shot him a quizzical glance. "Sure."

He turned on the television and flipped through the channels, stopping when he found the right station. Then he clicked off the screen to darken the room.

The smooth sound of jazz filled the suite. Jack approached her from behind, placing his hands on her shoulders and kissing her neck. The sultry music mingled with the brush of his kisses and her soft gasp. She tensed at his touch.

"Relax," he urged.

But his words had the opposite effect. How could she relax when the things she'd been fantasizing about doing with this man for the past week were about to become a reality? His nearness made her senses spin.

Standing behind her, Jack trailed his fingers up the length of Carrie's arms, then over her shoulders. They hesitated at the base of her neck, and for a moment she thought he was going to unzip her dress. But then he reached around to give her a tender squeeze.

"Are you sure this is what you want?" He was a gentleman to ask, but she thought it was a ludicrous question. Truth be told, she had never been more sure of anything.

"Yes."

He let out a breath. "Since the moment you walked into the restaurant tonight, all I could think about was touching you, being touched by you." His hand skimmed the side of her breast. "I want to make this moment last."

"Anticipation." She leaned back against his hard chest, at last understanding the silent elevator ride. It was so hot. She reached around and let her fingers dance along the sides of his taut thighs, daring to graze across the front of his jeans. "I like it."

"Anticipation is the most exciting part," Jack agreed, his voice a husky whisper. His hands seared a slow path through the valley of her cleavage, down her abdomen, and then lower still. Her body swelled with desire. She leaned her head against his collarbone. His fingers caressed her, and she groaned. He kissed her neck again and whispered in her ear, "What else do you like? Do you like this?"

"Yes, Jack. Please."

"Come with me…" Taking her by the hand, he led her into the bedroom. The curtains were drawn, and the room was dark. He closed the bedroom door, and the music faded into the background.

"Jack." Carrie sat on the edge of the bed. "I can't see a thing."

"Good." He knelt before her; their faces were mere inches apart. "Don't try to see me." He kissed her lips. "Don't try to guess what's going to happen next." He kissed her again, this time, longer, harder. "Just go with it, baby. Anticipate it."

She exhaled as his lips trailed their way down her neck to her chest. This time, when his hands reached behind her, she heard the zipper of her dress begin to descend.

The dress dropped around her waist on the bed, and Jack eased her onto her back. She closed her eyes, allowing her other senses to take over as she sank onto the soft, plush bedding.

Carrie had never experienced such a fire building within her. She was holding on to control by a thread, and they had just begun. She couldn't see him, only feel his lips and tongue on her stomach and his hands caressing her skin, touching her breasts, sliding over her trembling thighs.

Why was she so anxious?

It wasn't as if she'd never been with a man before. But this was different. There was something forbidden about this interlude, and it made her very nervous.

But very, very hot.

"You look so beautiful right now," Jack said. Her eyes fluttered open to find his silhouette hovering over her in the darkness. He unbuttoned his shirt and eased it off in one slow but fluid motion.

He dropped to his knees at the foot of the bed, his body wedged between her open legs. "I can't wait to taste you," he murmured. "But not yet. We'll get to that."

She shuddered at the promise. Jack leaned forward, his hands pushing the straps of her lacy black bra off her shoulders. He pulled the dainty undergarment down around her waist, not bothering to unclasp it. A moment later, his mouth was on her breast, circling her taut nipple with his tongue. She cried out when he nipped it, pleasure already beginning to surge through her limbs.

She sat up and met his hungry lips. Her breasts pressed against his bare, muscular chest. She pulled her body forward to the edge of the bed, chest heaving with anticipation. He deepened their kiss. Carrie's mind went numb when he sucked on her lower lip.

He pulled her to her feet, and the dress shimmied down her legs to the floor. She reached around and unhooked her bra, revealing herself to him in nothing but a pair of black lace panties. His eyes burned into her.

He unbuckled his belt and pulled it through the loops. Even silhouetted in darkness, his body was damn near perfect. Everything about him was hard and toned, from his broad shoulders to his washboard abs. He unbuttoned his dark jeans. She licked her lips as he unzipped them, the sound of the zipper scraping strangely erotic. He left his boxer shorts on as the jeans came off, sliding down his muscular legs to the floor.

"Jack..." She arched forward, aching with her own need.

He kicked off his pants and dropped onto the bed, taking her with him. She landed on top. The rigid length of his erection pressed against her thigh, and she sashayed against it, drawing from him a delicious groan.

If she was going to do this, she was not about to leave any room for regrets. Carrie wanted to experience every part of him. "I want to taste you," she said, sprinkling kisses across his abdomen as she worked her way down his hard body. Her hair fell forward, spilling across his skin as she hovered above. She tucked it behind her ears. "Right now."

She lowered her head and drew a path from his chest to the waistband of his boxer shorts with her tongue. She couldn't get enough. His taste, his scent, his smooth velvet skin. The man intoxicated her.

Jack groaned as she tugged the thin material down his hips and tossed the boxers onto the floor. Her mouth descended upon him.

Carrie had touched him before and knew he was big, but the feel of his cock in her mouth was startling. It took a moment for her to adjust to the sensation, then, breathing through her nose, she glided her lips along his shaft. She widened her jaw and took him all the way to the back of her throat. He groaned again, his fingers diving into her hair. She pulled back and circled her tongue around the tip, then slid her mouth down his length again, taking him all the way in.

With a frustrated growl, he pulled her away. "Baby, if you don't stop, I swear I'll explode right now. And I don't want to go there without you."

Carrie released a slow, raspy laugh that sent a ripple of breath across the hairs on his chest. "Then tell me what you want."

"I'd rather show you."

Jack wasn't kidding when he'd said he wanted to take things slow. His lips slithered down her body, his mouth pausing again over the soft swell of her breasts. She moaned with pleasure as he circled her nipples with his tongue. She felt them tighten, rigid with her want for him. Winding her arms around his back, she pulled him closer. He gave her nipple a final tug with his teeth before reclaiming her mouth.

Carrie rose to meet him. She was seized by an overwhelming need to be as close to him as possible. She thrust her tongue deeper into his mouth, desperate for more. Their bodies ground against each other; his hands were everywhere.

"God, Carrie, you feel so good." His breath was short as he ended the kiss. "Close your eyes."

She complied, letting her eyes drift shut as Jack untangled his body from hers. Still, unable to relinquish full control of the situation, she listened to his movements, trying to figure out what he was doing and anticipate what was next.

She heard the rustle of his clothes. Was he getting dressed? No, of course not. Carrie turned her head to the side, a wrinkle in her forehead. What was that sound? He was opening his wallet. She heard the rip of foil. *Oh yes.* He had brought a condom.

Jack hooked his fingers under the lace band of her panties and eased them off. She sighed with satisfaction as the weight of his body settled onto hers.

"Are you ready?" He spread her thighs with his, hovering over her with his strong forearms on either side of her head. She was hyper-aware of every spot their bodies made contact as they melded together. Her breasts pressed against his chest, their hips bound together, even his hair brushing over her forehead.

"I'm beyond ready." She ran her fingernails up his back.

Jack sank into her with one deep, driving thrust. She gasped. Though she was ready for him, nothing could have prepared her for the power of their union.

For a moment they were still. Then Jack began to rock inside of her, moving in a rhythm that sent them both spiraling. She raised her knees and wrapped her ankles around the backs of his thighs, driving him deeper into her heat. He pumped harder and faster. A slow tingle blossomed in her core and then spread through her body like wildfire until she unraveled around him.

"Come on, baby," he urged between ragged breaths. "I need to hear you come."

It didn't take long. She shouted his name, shuddering in his arms. With a low, animal groan and one final, frenzied thrust, Jack's own release ripped through his body. He collapsed against her, both lost in pleasure.

Carrie snuggled against him, listening to the sound of his heart beating like a wild drum. Sex with Jack had been even more incredible than she ever dared to imagine. She'd been fantasizing about him all week, and to her amazement, the reality turned out to be more incredible than the fantasy.

But as she nestled deeper into his embrace, one question screeched through her mind. Now that she'd been with Jack Dillon, how would she ever be able to let him go?

Just your body, she warned herself sternly. *Don't let him take your heart, too.*

****

"Good morning."

Carrie's eyes fluttered open to find Jack leaning over her in bed. The five o'clock shadow he wore the evening before had deepened in the night. She smiled at the sight of his face.

He placed a gentle kiss on her lips. "Sleep well?"

"Uh-huh."

"No regrets?" he asked, his tone light but the question blunt.

Her smile widened. "Nope."

"Good." He kissed her again, scratching her cheek with the gruff hair on his face. Carrie loved the feel of it, the feel of him.

She sat up as Jack rose from the bed, forcing a smile to mask her disappointment. "Are you leaving?"

"We have a staff meeting at nine," he reminded her, running a hand through his sleep-tousled hair. She glanced at the alarm clock on her bedside table. It was six thirty.

"I'm going to jump in the shower here, if you don't mind, then run home to get dressed." With a smirk, he added, "I can't run a staff meeting in the clothes I wore last night."

His gaze dropped to her exposed breasts. On instinct, she started to pull the sheet to conceal them but forced herself to stop. With Jack, she didn't want to be the woman who covered up. So she sat on the bed, her only armor the white sheet tangled around her legs. "Sounds great."

Carrie's gaze followed his retreat into the bathroom. She smiled at the sight of his perfect bare ass.

When the bathroom door clicked shut behind him, she flopped against the pillow and pulled the sheet over her chest. After their night of passion, how was she going to make it through a day of business as usual? Could she really sit across from him at their staff meeting and pretend like nothing happened while at the same time fantasizing about climbing on the conference room table and pulling Jack up there with her?

The hiss of the shower turning on drifted from the bathroom, and her brows scrunched together. She hoped he wasn't having second thoughts about what they were doing. Last night their decision to be together had been driven by lust and wine and her excitement at being in Las Vegas. They promised each other two weeks, no strings attached. But now that they had spent the night together, she couldn't help but wonder if Jack would want to continue with their plan.

He answered her question a moment later when the bathroom door opened, and he stepped out. Behind him, steam from the shower swirled around the room, forming a steamy backdrop for the flawless silhouette of his naked body. He was fully aroused and not even hiding the fact.

"Well," he said, beckoning her with a mischievous smile, "are you joining me in here or not?"

Chapter Eight

It was not yet nine when Carrie arrived in the conference room for their morning staff meeting. She was surprised to find Mark at the table, a laptop and a stream of papers spread in front of him.

"Good morning." She placed her new Louis Vuitton on the opposite end of the table. Her morning tryst in the shower with Jack still had her smiling more than two hours later. "You're in early."

Mark raised his head and looked at her with tired eyes. His short hair was mussed, and Carrie noticed his tie was loosened around the neck. "More like working late," he said. "I've been here all night going through the budget. Jack wants to see numbers before the end of the day." He gestured toward the credenza behind him. "There's coffee if you're interested."

"Thanks." Carrie wandered over and filled a mug. Steam drifted up and the coffee's rich aroma danced around her. She inhaled deeply and smiled at Mark, feeling more than a little guilty knowing he was working all night while she and Jack had been banging the hell out of each other a few floors below.

"You must be tired," she said, joining him at the table. "I think I lost the stamina for pulling all-nighters back in college. I hope I'm not disturbing you."

"No, I could use the break." Mark rubbed his eyes.

Carrie had not noticed the gray around his temples

117

before. Studying him in the bright sunlight streaming in through the open blinds, Mark looked older than Carrie initially pegged him to be. She wondered if he was married.

"Funny how you see a person every day, but you don't really know anything about them outside of work," Carrie mused. "Have you always lived in Las Vegas?"

"No, I'm from Los Angeles. Been here since '88."

"You must like it," she said, glancing out the window to the Strip below. From her thirtieth-floor vantage point, she could see clear across the city to the desert and mountains beyond. "I don't know if I could ever see myself living here for any real length of time."

"You'd be surprised," Mark said. "It's a great place if you can stand the heat. Everything is new and clean and wide-open. But tough to make friends. People here tend to be very untrusting."

She turned from the window to face him, realizing as she did Mark was staring at her. He looked away. "I don't know," she said. "Everyone I've met has been very nice. Sherry and Jack, you...I think you're all great people."

"That's different," he said. "I mean real friends. Jack and I have been good friends for a few years, but I can honestly say he's the one person in this city who I trust. Seems like everyone else here is looking to get something."

Carrie considered his words for a moment, not wanting to believe them. After a moment, she asked, "Are you married?"

Mark let out a bitter sound, half-laughter and half-grunt. "To who? A cocktail waitress or a gold digger?

Those are pretty much my options at this point in life."

"What are you talking about?" Carrie smiled, brushing off his self-deprecation. "You're a good-looking man. I bet women fall all over you."

"Women fall all over men like Jack," he said, but his voice reflected no bitterness. "I'm just the old guy who manages his casino."

"You're selling yourself short."

Mark shook his head in disagreement. "I'm not complaining. I've been in Vegas for a long time, seen everything there is to see. I'm not cut out to do anything else in life. I love my job, but when it comes to women...the cards have never been stacked in my favor."

She offered him a sympathetic smile.

Mark continued, "When you're young and just starting out, you think the whole world is in your hands. You think there's time for all those things down the road. But take it from me, when you see a chance at love, grab on and don't let go."

Carrie shivered at his words. Though they had spent time together outside of work, Mark was still little more than a stranger. Yet his words hit her with the same impact as if an old friend had spoken them. Was her heart that transparent?

She took a long, thoughtful sip of coffee. "Do you regret your life here?"

Before Mark could answer, the door to the conference room opened and Jack entered, a Starbucks cup in his hand. The three exchanged greetings. As more members of Jack's staff filed into the room for their morning meeting, Mark stood and gathered his belongings.

"I'm heading home to get some sleep," Mark told them. "I'll have the budget for you this afternoon, Jack."

As he exited the conference room, Mark stopped and leaned in to whisper in Carrie's ear. "Life is too short for regrets." He raised his eyebrows in Jack's direction.

"What was that all about?" Jack asked, sitting in his chair at the head of the conference room table as the door swung shut behind Mark.

Carrie smiled into her coffee mug. "Nothing."

****

Having only the cab ride from the airport to her hotel as a frame of reference, Carrie had no idea Las Vegas could be so pretty beyond the urban chaos of the Strip. But sitting beside Jack as he drove from the Grand Portofino to his house left her awestruck. She took in the beauty of the Nevada landscape through the window of his Audi.

It was his idea to get away from the Strip for a quiet evening alone. Keeping their relationship a secret was no easy task. Around almost every corner at the hotel, they bumped into a familiar face, and sooner or later, people would start wondering why they were spending so much time together.

It was the magic hour just before twilight, when the sun burned over the horizon, streaking the sky in a flaming pattern of red and orange. Rocks and cacti jutted from the ground, dark silhouettes against the dying sun. Carrie had never seen such vast openness. As they drove down the two-lane highway, there was nothing but the desert stretching to the east and west.

When Jack pulled into a residential neighborhood,

the sudden appearance of homes surprised her. The gated community seemed set in the middle of nowhere. She peered through the window. Large, expensive-looking houses hugged the perimeter of a golf course, the rolling green hills a stark but tranquil contrast to the brown desert landscape they had driven past on their way. It was all so different from her world in New York City, like night and day.

"What a beautiful house." Carrie gazed at the tan two-story stucco facade as Jack pulled into his driveway. He parked and stepped around to open the passenger side door for her.

He popped the trunk and removed a bag of groceries they had stopped along the way to buy. With the paper bag balanced under one arm, he led Carrie up the walkway with the other. Neat rows of flowers lined the front of his house, filling the warm evening air with their fragrant scent. The landscaping was flawless. She was certain he had professionals maintaining the impressive property.

Jack unlocked the door and waved her in first. She scanned their surroundings as he followed her into the house, his hand on the small of her back. A curved staircase sprawled upward before them, and to the left, a living room larger than Carrie's whole apartment in New York. The room was sparsely furnished, with a pair of couches and a liquor cabinet, and a wall unit housing a giant flat-screen TV and stereo. She could still smell the fresh paint.

"I just moved in a month ago," Jack said in way of explanation, reading the expression on her face. "Haven't had time to decorate yet."

Carrie set her purse on one of the couches. "I like

your sofas. They're such a pretty color." She ran her fingers over the soft beige fabric. Though she tried to do the polite thing and say something positive, a heaviness settled on her heart. The vast emptiness of the room overwhelmed her.

"It could probably use a woman's touch," he said, not looking her in the eye. "I don't get to spend much time here."

Carrie followed him into the kitchen. In contrast to the living room, Jack's oversized kitchen was a dream. Granite countertops gleamed under dark maple cabinets, and the stainless steel appliances were new and top of the line. The entire room possessed a classy, southwestern appeal. She ran her hand over the smooth, cool surface of the island that dominated the space.

Jack removed a pot from a cabinet and filled it with water for the pasta. He was still in his tailored suit pants and white dress shirt, though the tie had come off and his sleeves were rolled up. The juxtaposition of the hotel mogul standing in his homey kitchen made her head tumble. He looked so damn good.

What had Jack said last night? Anticipation was the most exciting part. He wasn't kidding; she was already yearning for him. She longed to kiss him, to have him inside of her. Clutching her, moving with her, burying his beautiful cock deep inside her the way he had last night. Pure and raw.

She shook away the sensation and looked around the kitchen for something less X-rated to fill the void in her mind.

"Oh, who drew these?" she asked, rushing over to the side-by-side refrigerator where two colorful construction paper pictures hung. In childlike handwriting, one of them said, in bold red crayon, "We miss you, Uncle Jack!" It had a picture of a family standing in front of a house. The other, equally colorful and childlike, had a bright yellow sun in the corner of the page, shining down on a Crayola-brown puppy standing in the grass.

He glanced at the fridge from where he stood by the island. His face broke into a bright, proud smile when he saw the pictures. "My nieces in Ohio."

"I didn't know you had family back east."

"My brother and his clan."

Carrie unpacked the groceries, his gaze burning into her from where he stood by the stove. She glanced over to find the hint of a quirky smile on his face. She winked at him, then opened the fridge door and placed the chicken they had bought into the glass meat drawer.

Jack's gaze set once again on the little girls' drawings when she closed the fridge door. "I don't see them much," he mused. "My mom is in California, and my brother still lives in Toledo. They're the only family I have."

"Where's your dad?"

Jack's gaze dropped from the drawings to the kitchen island, where he was about to start chopping carrots. "He's dead."

Carrie stopped in her tracks, realizing how uncomfortable she had made him. "I'm sorry, Jack. I didn't mean to pry."

He laid the knife on the wooden cutting board and turned to her. "You weren't prying. I guess I'm not used to talking about my personal life with other people."

"How did he die?"

His voice was low but composed. "Car accident. I was five, but my mom told me years later there was another woman in the car with him. That's how she found out he'd been having an affair."

"Oh my God."

"No kidding." Jack let out a long breath. "He was a very successful lawyer, made a lot of money, and there were always women throwing themselves at him. The guy didn't know how to say no." He was silent for a moment, a faraway look on his face. Then he shook his head as if snapping back to reality. "Anyway, it was just the three of us growing up. I see them now a couple of times a year, but business keeps me so busy. You know how it is."

Guilt bubbled through her as Carrie realized family was a sore subject for Jack. But hearing about them opened a window into his soul she would have never otherwise discovered. She placed a comforting hand on his shoulder as he returned to chopping the vegetables.

"Do you want to talk about it?"

"No, actually, I don't." Jack placed the knife on the counter and went into the living room, leaving her to stare after him from beside the stove. She looked at the abandoned cutting board and bit her lip, wishing she could lighten the mood.

"Can I get you a drink?" Jack called. Carrie moved to the doorway and watched as he removed a bottle of scotch from the liquor cabinet and poured a drink.

"I'll wait until dinner."

He jostled the glass to give his drink a stir, then took a long sip.

"I didn't mean to upset you," she said, disappointed the evening had taken a melancholy turn.

The glass paused in midair. "I'm not upset." Jack looked at her and his voice softened. "It's just been a long time since I thought about my father."

Carrie nodded. She didn't like talking about her parents, either. She and Jack barely knew each other, yet at this moment, he was the closest person to her in the world. She ached for him when he told her about his father's death, respected his obvious love for his brother and nieces. Just like last night at the piano bar, the way she had filled with pride when he told her how he built his business from nothing more than a few good ideas and wise investments. There was a connection between them so much deeper than the one week they'd known each other should in any way allow.

She yearned to open the doors to her own heart for Jack to peer in and see. There was so much she wanted to share, about her own childhood and past loves, but she resisted the urge. It was one thing to hear him talk about his past but letting him into her head would be too dangerous. They only had a few weeks together, and they'd agreed their time would be about sex, about excitement and passion and fun. To allow emotions to deepen their bond would confuse the matter.

"I didn't mean to be nosey." Carrie crossed into the living room and placed her hand on his arm. "Maybe it's best if we don't talk about our pasts with each other."

"You weren't being nosey," Jack said, meeting her gaze. They sat on the couch. "But we don't have to get too personal if that's the way you want it."

She squeezed his arm, then took her hand away. It wasn't what she wanted, but it was what she had to settle for. She wanted him, all of him. Her ideal man. And she knew the only thing stopping them from being together was her own ambition. But it wasn't a blind ambition. She was sensible enough to realize pursuing anything more with Jack would be career suicide. She could have his body, but not his heart and soul.

"What do you think of this house?" His unexpected question snapped Carrie's attention to him.

"I told you. I think it's…nice."

He turned to her on the couch. "Tell me what you really think."

She looked around the living room. Light from the kitchen splattered onto the barren white wall under the staircase. The front of the room had a wall of windows, and Carrie imagined they must let in dazzling light during the day. But right now the blinds were drawn shut. No curtains adorned them. In fact, there wasn't much of anything by way of decoration in the room. Not even artwork hanging on the wall.

"I think it's a lot of space for one person. I think it's—"

"Lonely." He completed the sentence for her.

"I was about to say 'showy.' I think you are so concerned with what other people's perceptions of Jack Dillon are, you forget who you *really* are."

"And who am I?"

"Well, my opinion is just another perception. You need to figure it out for yourself." She looked around the near-empty room. It reminded her of her sister Jill's formal living room in Connecticut. Pristine to the naked eye, but void of any life. She kept the kids' toys stored in the family room, and nobody ever went in there except on special occasions. It was a wasted space. "I think everyone assumes Jack Dillon should live in a big house in a fancy neighborhood, so you do. But are you happy here?"

"I used to think so." His voice was low and weighted with regret. "Now, it just feels very big and empty."

Carrie stood at a loss for words. Hadn't they agreed not to get personal? And yet somehow, as much as she fought it, it felt natural to be the person Jack confided in. She took his hand. "Why do you think it feels that way?"

"Well, take my brother Doug," Jack said. "I can't tell you how many times I've offered to move him out here, offered him a job at any hotel he wanted. But he won't do it. I used to think he was crazy for wanting to stay in Ohio. I know he can't be making very much money at his job now. But lately, when I think about him there with his wife and his kids, I can't believe how jealous it makes me."

She nodded in understanding. "It's the same for me. For so long, all I wanted was to prove my independence and have a career and a place of my own. And now I have those things—and I'm so close to making partner—but for some reason, I still want more."

"Do you want kids?"

"Very much, but not right away. And not if it means losing my entire identity outside of being a wife and mother and having nothing more challenging to do in life than ironing my husband's shirts and remembering which day was my turn to drive the carpool."

"I'd like to have kids someday, too," he confided.

"Does that surprise you?"

"Not at all." She smiled, remembering the way his whole face had lit up talking about his nieces. "I think everyone has the same instincts at some point in life."

She turned to him on the couch, making the decision to share just a little bit more. "When I think about my mom, it's hard to imagine she was already married and had two kids by my age. There's so much pressure from my parents to get married, start a family, and be more like my sister." She shook her head. "I just can't see myself married to a man who doesn't respect my independence, but sometimes I still think it would have been easier to marry David and get everyone off my back."

"No." Jack pushed away a stray tendril of hair from against her cheek. "Don't sell yourself short to make other people happy. You're too strong of a person to go there."

Carrie smiled at him, grateful for the praise. She couldn't remember the last time she had somebody in her corner. "I think that's the best compliment anyone has ever given me."

A comfortable silence washed over the room. She had never talked about her parents' expectations for her with anyone before, let alone how much those expectations went against the grain of what she wanted out of life. She felt closer to Jack now but suddenly very vulnerable. Being with him was so easy; opening up to him seemed natural and right. But at the same time, she had to remember their agreement. This affair was about sex, not friendship.

She stood, remembering the pasta primavera they were going to cook. "I think the water is boiling."

****

Dinner turned into a sexually charged affair. Jack poured a heaping serving of pasta onto one big plate, and they shared the meal at the kitchen island, barstools pulled close and feet hooked together under the counter. They took turns feeding each other forkfuls, talking and laughing until every last bite was gone.

Now, Jack watched Carrie from the arched doorway separating his living room from the kitchen. He was amazed by the serene beauty she exuded as she stood at the sink washing dishes, humming to herself, oblivious to the tenderness in his gaze. Her hair was piled high in a messy bun. Despite air-conditioning, the kitchen had grown warm from the cooking.

He hadn't meant to tell her about his brother or the sordid way his dad had died. His private life was something Jack typically protected with the force of a lion's roar, but tonight it would have felt wrong *not* to share with her.

Though he wanted Carrie to share more in return, the little bit that broke through her cool exterior tonight was promising.

Part of him wished she had spoken more about David, but he'd been careful not to push or risk making her uncomfortable by asking. The other part of him was glad she didn't; her ex-fiancé sounded like a total douche, and hearing about how he treated this smart, independent, driven woman made him want to pop the guy in the head.

Jack drifted over to the sink and placed a hand on the base of Carrie's long, graceful neck. He was done thinking about his dad, Doug, David, and everyone else on the planet, for that matter. Right now, he wanted to focus on her.

"Hi." He brushed his lips against the side of her neck.

"Hi." She tilted her head and sighed, almost giggling with pleasure.

His tongue explored the delicate spot between neck and ear. His voice was hoarse as he whispered, "You look so damn good in my kitchen."

"Kind of sexist, don't you think?" Carrie raised a playful eyebrow and turned to look at him.

"I guess that did come out a little more 1950s suburban housewife than I intended." He chuckled, nibbling on her ear. "But you do look good."

He pressed his body against her, pinning Carrie to the kitchen counter. Her hands still hung immersed in the soapy pot she'd been scrubbing in the sink, forgotten for the moment. With another soft moan of delight, she tilted her head back against his white button-down shirt.

He reached around and tightened his grasp, holding her so close the warmth of her skin seared through the light fabric of her sundress. His lips caressed the exposed skin on her neck, whispering her name between kisses. He ran a hand slowly down the front of her body, from her collarbone, through the dip of her cleavage, and over her dress to her stomach. She felt so damn good.

Carrie loosened his grip and turned in his arms until they stood face to face. Her smoldering eyes locked with his. She grasped him with her wet, soapy hands, leaving trails of white bubbles on his forearms. Their skin glided together under the wetness.

With a groan, Jack crushed his mouth to hers. As

she reached to circle her arms around his neck, he slid his tongue across her lips. Teasing her. Tasting her. Wanting her like he had never wanted anyone before.

"I've been thinking about this moment all day," he whispered against her ear. "I can't wait to fuck you. I want to hear you scream my name."

She gasped at his dirty words. But she leaned into their embrace, the swell of her perfect tits crushing against his chest. He slid his hands down the small of her back, eager to touch the soft, bare flesh that had been tempting him since they left the hotel. He found it just below the hem of her sundress, on the firm, smooth backs of her thighs.

The sound of running water filled the room, but the dishes were long forgotten. Still locked in an embrace, Jack spun them around until his back was to the sink, then moved with Carrie a few steps across the kitchen, pinning her petite frame between his body and the refrigerator. The kitchen was hot, and they were making it hotter.

Reaching around her, he pressed the button of the ice maker. Two cubes tumbled out and landed in his hand.

She gasped in surprise when he pressed the ice to her thigh, trailing it up her leg, over her lace panties, and onto her back. Water drizzled down her skin, and she shivered from more than the cold. Then he moved his hand around to the front and pressed the ice to her collarbone, watching the water trail down the curve of her breast and disappear beneath the front of her sundress. The sound of her soft moans made him rock hard. He pressed his body into her.

Jack slipped what was left of the melting wedge of

ice between her lips. She leaned forward to recapture his mouth, the slip of ice melting as it moved between them. It took all his willpower to end the sensual embrace. He pulled away, stilling his wandering hands and lips. He was dying to be inside her, but it was not quite time.

Carrie's eyes widened in surprise when she saw his expression. "What's the matter?"

"Nothing, beautiful." He smiled and ran a hand over her soft hair. "Anticipation, remember?"

"Jack, please," she pleaded. "I don't think I can wait any longer."

His expression turned serious. "You know, I feel a little guilty bringing you here to my house, knowing all along this whole evening was leading to one thing."

"Isn't that what we agreed on?"

"Yes, but…you deserve better."

"Are you saying you want to stop?" Her voice held a pout, and she ground her hips against his hard-on in a bold attempt to convince him otherwise.

He shook his head, his eyes locked on hers. He was playing a game. Even though his balls were screaming in protest, he wanted to make her wait. Her protests only made him more determined to drive her crazy with anticipation, knowing the sex would be even more explosive. He gave her a wicked smile. "I have a better idea."

Carrie tilted her head, waiting to hear his plan. In one sweeping motion, he swept her into his arms. She whooped in surprise. Then, carrying her from the kitchen, he announced, "I think we could both use a good cooling off."

Chapter Nine

"Are you sure this is a good idea?"

"Trust me, Carrie," Jack said. "It's a *great* idea."

Jack pulled a key card from his wallet. They were back at the hotel, slipping into one of the private villas the Grand Portofino reserved for high rollers and A-list guests. It was the last place she expected to be at ten o'clock at night, but Jack was full of surprises.

"Then why do I feel like we're doing something wrong?" She kept her voice low and stuck close to his side as he unlocked the door. Holding hands, they slipped inside.

"I promise we won't get kicked out," he whispered, flipping on the lights. He gave her a wink. "I know the owner."

Carrie let go of his hand and wandered around the villa's posh living room, taking in the expensive furnishings, colorful artwork, and glossy full kitchen. The sweet smell of vanilla permeated the air. "It's so beautiful."

"So are you," Jack said. When she met his gaze, he was smiling. "I thought maybe you'd like to move in for the rest of your stay in Vegas."

"Into this villa?" She looked around the extravagant room again.

"Yeah," Jack said, as if a ten thousand dollar a night villa was no big deal. Never mind the living room alone was bigger than her entire studio apartment in New York City. "Why not?"

"It's a little more space than I need." She shook her head. Even the suite upstairs was a decadent treat; she would have been content staying in a regular room, as long as it had a desk and strong Wi-Fi. She wouldn't even know what to do in a villa this luxurious.

"Don't decide yet." He took her hand again. "Let me show you the pool. I promised you a swim."

"Okay."

He led her across the villa's living room and through a pair of French doors onto the patio. "You're not still nervous, are you?" He glanced at her over his shoulder and gave the hand he was holding a playful little shake.

"Of course not," she lied, brushing away the notion with a smile.

Wary at first of going back to the hotel together when he suggested a dip in the villa's hot tub, she had finally agreed. They drove to the Grand Portofino from Jack's house, and she went to her room to grab a swimsuit and change while he stopped by the front desk for a key to the villa. She would have preferred to stay at his house, but he was keen on a little adventure, and she didn't want to disappoint.

Stepping outside onto the private patio, Carrie smiled at the sight. A small rectangular swimming pool filled most of the space, flanked by a whirlpool tub and two cushioned lounge chairs. Behind the chairs, a stack of thick, white towels sat ready.

Jack slipped off his shoes and the Ohio State Buckeyes sweatshirt he'd thrown on at his house and placed them on one of the lounge chairs. Carrie, too, stripped to her white swimsuit and placed her clothes next to his on the chair.

Her gaze followed Jack as he approached the hot tub's control panel. He turned the dial, and the jets sprang to life. He descended the steps and sat on the bench, and she drank in the ripple of muscles that defined his broad chest.

"Coming in?" He leaned back on his elbows.

She followed him into the water, stepping on the first step and sitting on the edge. The cool ceramic tiles against her thighs and rear end created a startling contrast to the hot water bubbling around her feet.

Carrie looked around, wishing she could extinguish the stubborn flicker of apprehension. Although they were alone in the villa's private garden, the hotel's tower loomed above them, where anyone could look down from a window and see. "I think we need to be super careful about where we go together. I don't want anyone to catch us."

"We're just going for a little swim." He gave her a lighthearted splash. "There's no crime happening here. Besides," he added, leaning against the wall of the spa, "doesn't the prospect of getting caught turn you on just a little bit?"

Carrie considered his words. A resounding "no" echoed through her head. She appreciated his taste for adventure but wished he could understand why she was so adamant about not getting caught. If he had his way, they'd be flaunting their arrangement to everyone. He was Jack Dillon, owner of this damn hotel. It was not in his nature to accept having to sneak around.

She gazed up at the inky blue sky and half-full moon peeking out from between the hotel towers. The moonlight splashed down through the palm trees above them, creating a shadow of jagged patterns across the water and top of her bare thighs.

"Come here." His voice lowered to a growl. Shadows from the palm trees above danced across his outstretched arms.

She didn't want to spoil the mood with her apprehension. Right now, she just wanted to finish what they had begun in the kitchen.

She slid into the water as Jack moved toward her. They met in the middle, bodies colliding with a gentle splash, and she wrapped her arms around his neck. His mouth covered hers.

His lips were warm and slick from the rising steam, rousing in Carrie a passion that grew stronger with every moment. He slipped an arm under her knees, then scooped her into his arms. With their lips still locked together, Jack spun through the water and sat on the bench of the spa, pulling her onto his lap.

She sighed as he pulled her body close, searing a path down his neck and across his chest with her lips. Her long blonde hair swished against him, fanning out as it floated in the spa's cascade of bubbles. She dipped her head back, submerging her whole head underwater for a moment, and then rose from the water. Her wet hair was sleek against her scalp.

At the sight, Jack let out a savage groan. The sound of his wanting left her dizzy with desire, awed to have the power to draw that groan from this man.

She waded away through the water, slipping from his reach. He stared, his expression like a boy who just had his candy taken away. But then Carrie gave him a coy, inviting smile. She slid the white straps of her bathing suit off her shoulders and down her arms, revealing to him her wet, bare breasts.

"I love it when you smile at me that way." Jack pushed off the bench and glided through the water, meeting her in the center of the spa. He skimmed a finger over her neck and collarbone, tracing her nipples and the swell of her full breasts. She sighed appreciatively, and he lowered his mouth over one pert nipple, swirling his tongue over her tender flesh.

Carrie let her hand venture underwater, finding him erect and pressing against the thin fabric of his swim shorts. She wrapped her hand around him and gasped when in response he bit her nipple. But the sensation was more sensual than painful, and she began to stroke his length.

Jack groaned, then recaptured her mouth in a searing kiss. Without releasing her from their passionate embrace, he slid his hand down her back and over the curve of her ass. His finger pressed against her most sensitive spot, and she arched against him.

With that encouragement, he slipped his hand under the elastic of her swimsuit and continued to touch her. Carrie broke away and pressed her face against the inside of his neck, her body on fire with pleasure. She moaned again as he slipped his fingers inside her. Under the water, her hips moved in sync with his rhythmic, pulsing touch, sending her right to the edge of ecstasy.

Was it the danger of getting caught adding to the excitement? Maybe Jack was right, after all. They were alone, but anyone looking out their window from the hotel tower above might see. Her heart pumped with adrenaline. She had never been with a man outdoors before.

She slid her mouth up his neck and against his ear. "I want you now," she said, tasting the sharp sting of chlorine on his skin. He was killing her tonight, making her wait, delaying the inevitable just for the fun of it.

"Are you sure?"

"God, yes. Please." She ran her hand down his toned chest to the waistband of his shorts and reached inside, holding his gaze with clear intentions.

Carrie tugged his shorts, but the swish of the French doors flying open jolted their attention upward. Startled, they looked up to find Sherry emerging onto the patio from the villa with a sheepish smile on her face.

Jack swore under his breath. Carrie dipped below the waterline, pulling the thin white straps of her swimsuit over her shoulders.

"Jack, I've been calling you all night." Sherry was out of breath when she reached them. She scanned the scene. "I'm so sorry to interrupt. The front desk told me you took a key to this room."

"What's the matter, Sherry?" he asked.

Carrie climbed the whirlpool steps and rushed to her side, grabbing one of the towels and wrapping it around her waist. Sherry's frantic state had her too alarmed to even think about the interruption or the implications of being caught with Jack.

"It's Mark," Sherry said.

Jack stayed in the water. His rock-hard erection had been in her hand not ten seconds ago, so Carrie knew it would be at least a few minutes before he could emerge from the spa. He looked at the two women looming over him. "What happened?"

"He's had a heart attack."

****

Carrie paced the hospital corridor, her damp hair pulled into an unkempt ponytail, waiting for the doctor to give them an update on Mark's condition. Sherry and Jack sat in silence in the row of bright orange plastic chairs that lined the waiting area.

At last, a doctor emerged from the unit. Jack and Sherry rose and joined her, demanding news of Mark's condition.

"What we've had here is a false alarm," the doctor said. "I think it's safe to say he will fully recover. Might want to pay a little closer attention to diet and exercise."

Jack nodded, accepting the news, a relieved expression brightening his tired face.

The doctor asked, "Does Mr. Jergens have a wife or any relatives who need to be contacted?"

Carrie looked at the linoleum-tiled floor with a sad expression.

"No," Jack said.

"Okay, well, we're going to keep him here tonight for observation. I think he'll be all right to go home in the morning, providing his condition stays stabilized and he takes at least a week off work to rest."

"You have my word," Jack promised. "Can we see him?"

The doctor surveyed the group. "Maybe just one of you. I don't want to get him too excited tonight."

"Why don't the two of you head home?" Jack suggested. "I'll visit Mark for a while and then catch a cab." The three of them had driven to the hospital together in Sherry's car.

If Sherry had known what they were doing in the spa, she didn't mention it during their drive back to the hotel, and Carrie was grateful. The two women rode in silence, sad and tired, but relieved Mark's condition was not too serious.

Carrie was fascinated by how Jack and his employees treated each other like family. The way this group of coworkers cared about each other warmed her heart. It was something she had never before experienced in all her years working in New York.

She was relieved when Sherry dropped her off near the valet stand in front of the Grand Portofino and did not offer to come with her. She was eager to be alone.

Once inside her suite, Carrie entered the lavish bathroom and turned on the shower, letting hot water wash away the events of the day. Poor Mark. Pangs of guilt rippled through her, harping on her problems while he lay alone in a hospital bed.

Remembering their earlier conversation, her heart filled with sympathy. It was obvious Mark was lonesome and had given up on finding love; now he had to face his recovery alone, too. She wished there was something she could do to brighten his spirits.

The room was thick with steam when she emerged from the shower, and she wiped the mirror with a hand towel to see her reflection. She studied her figure with a critical eye. Her skin was bronzed from the sun, and her hair had grown lighter, too. She turned to better gage her waistline and decided she'd better start watching what she ate before it grew anymore. Her body still held its hourglass shape, but all this dining out and fancy cooking was bound to start taking a toll.

Wearing a plush bathrobe with the hotel's logo on

it and combing her wet hair, a knock at the door startled her attention away from the mirror. Instinctively, she knew it was Jack. Though she hadn't been expecting him, Carrie was not surprised he decided to come up. She crossed the suite's living room and peeked through the peephole before opening the door.

He stood in the hall, still dressed in his swim shorts and Ohio State sweatshirt he had worn to the hospital, a five o'clock shadow gracing his chiseled jaw.

"You look tired," she said, waving him in. She clicked the door shut behind him. Though it had only been hours, it felt more like days since Jack picked her up for their dinner date at his house. "How's Mark?"

"He's doing okay." Fatigue had left deep shadows under his usually animated eyes.

"God." Carrie sank onto the sofa. "I couldn't stop thinking of him the whole time after we left the hospital. Life is so precious. You don't realize it until something like this happens."

"Kind of like what we were talking about the night we got stuck in the elevator," Jack reminded her.

Carrie hadn't thought of that. "I suppose you're right," she said, fidgeting with the ties of her robe. "I feel so bad for Mark, nobody to take care of him. How will he get by after he's discharged from the hospital?"

"I'll arrange for him to stay here at the hotel." He looked around Carrie's living room. "At least for the first week. He'll be more comfortable and won't have to worry about cooking or cleaning."

Carrie knew Jack was a kind person, but it wasn't until this moment she realized how truly *good* he was. "You're a wonderful friend to help Mark this way."

"Just doing what anyone would."

"That's the thing," she said. "I don't think anyone else would."

He sat on the sofa beside her and took her hand. It felt so strong and protective, wrapped over hers. Staring at their entwined fingers, Jack said, "Seeing Mark hooked up to all those tubes and machines." He shook his head in disbelief. "It makes you appreciate being alive and healthy. It reminds you to live every day to the fullest."

She swallowed hard but did not respond.

"This has all made me realize how much I care about you, Carrie."

She pulled her hand away. "Jack, don't…"

He held it in his firm grasp, not allowing her to let go. "I know we said this was just going to be for two weeks, but—"

"Please, Jack. Let's not confuse things."

"I never imagined how much you would come to mean to me," he finished.

Carrie paused as his words sank in, and then she squeezed his hand. "You mean a lot to me, too."

He rubbed the scruff on his face and released a tense chuckle. "This isn't how I imagined tonight would turn out, sitting here in shorts and smelling like a hospital ward. When I invited you to dinner at my place, I wanted the night to be perfect."

Carrie cupped her hand around Jack's gruff cheek and met his gaze. Her eyes clouded with the emotions filling her heart. "It is."

He gathered her into his arms and held her close for a long moment. Then he kissed her.

The gentle kiss melted Carrie in his arms. It held promise and meaning, and she wanted to believe it was real. She closed her eyes and allowed him to take the lead. It was late and they were alone. She didn't want to talk anymore. All she wanted to do was to make love to Jack.

****

Lying in the cradle of his arms, Carrie's mind raced long after the passion of their night together had come to a climactic end. Beside her, Jack slept peacefully, his light, rhythmic breathing the sole sound in the room.

She closed her eyes and pressed her body closer, snuggling deeper into his sleeping embrace. His muscular legs were tangled with hers under the thin sheet. She ran her toes up the length of his calf, feeling the light spring of hair tickle against her foot. Beneath her, Jack's bare chest rose and fell. His warm breath ruffled her hair.

Why couldn't they have met at another time, in another place? Things might have been different. Replaying their conversation in her mind, she wanted to believe it could be real. That they could have a future. But Jack was a romantic, so she would need to be the realistic one.

She couldn't help but think of Sherry again, rushing in to find them locked together in the villa's hot tub. It did not take a genius to figure out they were not conducting a business meeting half-naked at ten o'clock at night.

Prickles of stress crept across Carrie's chest. Under no circumstances could she allow her time with Jack to get in the way of the job she was in Las Vegas to do.

With a sigh, she abandoned any hope of falling asleep. Her mind was racing a hundred miles an hour.

She untangled her body from the warmth of Jack's embrace and slipped into the bathroom. After this long and eventful night, a hot bath sounded like the perfect stress-reliever.

It was becoming harder and harder to keep things in perspective. The better she got to know Jack, the more Carrie realized keeping their relationship strictly physical, not to mention a secret from his staff, was going to be impossible.

Stepping into the tub, she willed herself to relax and stop thinking about those things. She rubbed a washcloth over her legs, then rested her head back against the edge of the Roman bathtub.

Carrie did her best to push all nagging thoughts to the back of her mind. There would be time enough to worry about where this was going. If nothing else, she hoped the bath would make her sleepy, and then she could curl back into bed with Jack. It had been a crazy day from start to finish, but now it was late, and she thanked her lucky stars there would be no more drama tonight.

Chapter Ten

Carrie slipped into Cardini's, flipping on the lights and taking a good look around the empty restaurant. Construction was complete. Rich leather booths lined two walls, and small square tables covered in white linen sat haphazardly throughout the center. Dark wood tones created a warm and cozy atmosphere. The restaurant just needed a few final touches, and it would be a stunning setting for their press event next week.

She had spoken to Antonio Cardini several times on the phone this week, and knew once he arrived in Las Vegas tomorrow, much of her time would be spent preparing him for the media interviews.

Carrie removed her laptop from its case and rested it on one of the tables. As she waited for the computer to boot up, she rubbed her eyes. It was getting late, and she still had a lot of work to finish.

The last several days had flown by in a whirl. It was no easy task balancing her demanding work schedule with the time she devoted to spending with Jack. To everyone else, they were simply publicist and client, passing the day in a flurry of meetings and activity. But at night they slipped into their more familiar roles, ordering room service and eating their meals naked. Snuggled together on the sofa at Jack's house. Having amazing sex in the glass-enclosed shower in his master bathroom. And on his bed. And the kitchen table.

She smiled at memories. In the last week, they had made love more times than she could count. With Dave, sex had been more of a chore. An expectation she had to meet if she wanted to be his wife. His pleasure always outweighing hers. But with Jack, making love was sinfully indulgent. Before he came into her life, she never knew how much fun it could be. How intense and playful and how utterly satisfying. She had no inhibitions when they were together. She couldn't get enough of it—or him—for that matter.

Carrie found time to visit with Mark, too. Just this afternoon, she and Sherry had surprised him by bringing lunch to his suite. Although still recuperating, Mark was grateful for the company and enjoyed hearing about all the things he was missing at work. He promised to try and make it to the grand opening of Cardini's.

Mark was missing a good week, too, Carrie mused. To thank everyone for their hard work, last night Jack had taken the entire leadership team to dinner. Afterward, the group went to the Foundation Room, a trendy club at the top of the Mandalay Bay Resort. They talked and laughed, listened to music, and sipped overpriced cocktails while taking in the sweeping view of the glittering Las Vegas Strip at night.

And they had danced. Thinking about it now, in the dim light of Cardini's, Carrie smiled. She and Sherry had gotten down to the club's DJ like two college girls. And when a slow song came on, she danced with Jack.

She replayed the magical moments in her mind. The feel of his strong arms around her, her head against his chest, their secret locked away between them. It was easy for her to pretend the dance was innocent. After all, if Sherry could dance with Frank in the Foundation Room without anyone raising an eyebrow, why couldn't she dance with Jack? She knew how to play it cool.

But playing it cool and staying cool while these crazy emotions burrowed in her heart were two very different things. She willed herself to stay grounded in reality, making a conscious effort not to think about the future. Instead, she focused on the pleasures of the present. Jack seemed to be enjoying their time together as well, accepting her noncommittal attitude without argument. But the two weeks were flying by fast, and sooner or later, she'd have to brace for their inevitable goodbye.

Sitting at the table in Cardini's, Carrie was so deep in thought she didn't hear Jack approach from behind. "Thought I'd find you here."

She jumped at the unexpected sound of his voice. "You scared me."

"Always working so hard," he said, bending to drop a light kiss on her lips before sitting at the table beside her. "Have you thought any more about moving into the villa?"

"I don't know, Jack," she said. She was quite comfortable in her suite, and the thought of packing all her stuff just to move to another part of the hotel seemed like more trouble than it was worth. "I like where I am. That suite is more than enough room for me. Heck, I'd be happy in a regular room."

"But think of the private hot tub." He waggled his eyebrows.

She laughed. "We get more than enough privacy

between my suite and your place. Besides," Carrie added, "I'm only here for another week."

Jack sat up straight. "Okay," he said, dropping the subject. Carrie could see he was annoyed by the reminder. "I won't push."

She leaned in close, wanting to appease him. "I don't need a fancy villa, Jack. I just want to be here with you."

"I get it, no worries." He rose from the chair. "How about I steal you away for dinner tonight?"

"I can't," she said. "Too much to do before tomorrow."

"Oh, come on." Jack sighed. He stood behind her chair and rubbed her shoulders. "You could use a break."

Carrie tilted her head and indulged in the massage. The tension in her neck melted under Jack's strong hands as he worked his magic, and it stirred in her images of what other magic he could work with those hands. *Just one week left.*

"Maybe just a bite."

"What are you in the mood for?" he asked, his hands still in motion. "Frank told me about this new Thai place downtown."

"Ugh, I'm so sick of restaurants." Carrie pushed her hair aside so he could get a better angle. "Let's go back to your place tonight."

"Okay." Jack leaned in close enough for her to feel his breath tickle her ear. "Though I'm not sure how much cooking we'll get done."

"Let's grab takeout for dinner," she suggested. "Then we won't have to waste time cooking at all."

"More time for other things," Jack agreed, planting

a kiss on her cheek before straightening.

She smirked, glad they were on the same page. "Let me finish here and then we can go. I want to make sure everything is set before Antonio arrives tomorrow."

"I think you are stressing way too much about this. Everything will be fine." He stepped around the table and pulled out the chair next to Carrie. He wore the same charcoal-gray suit he had on the day they got stuck in the elevator. She smiled at the memory and wondered if he was wearing his Batman boxer shorts, too. She'd find out soon enough.

"I just want everything to go well."

"I have complete faith in you." He took her hand and gave it an affectionate squeeze. "Now go upstairs and change into something comfortable. Let's forget about work for one night and have a relaxing evening at home."

Home. The word sounded nice.

But it was Jack's home, not hers. And in a week she'd be saying goodbye and going back to her life in New York. Why was it getting harder and harder to remember?

****

"I should go back to the casino," Jack whispered. There was a mournful tone in his voice, and even in the darkness of his bedroom, Carrie could tell he didn't want to leave. She didn't want him to go, either.

They were tangled together in Jack's bed, basking in the afterglow, the Chinese takeout they had picked up for dinner still in its bag on the kitchen counter downstairs. They'd both been hungry for other things first.

"It's been a few nights since I've done my evening rounds. I'm sure people are wondering where I am." He stroked a strand of her blonde hair trailing across his pillow. She followed his hand through the side of her eye, and he gave her hair a playful little tug. "You've been quite the distraction."

Carrie propped her head in her hand, not quite convinced they were through yet. "Do you have to go?" She trailed a finger down the center of his chest. He was still breathing hard. Her bare breasts grazed against him as she leaned in a little closer.

"If I don't go now, we might never make it out of this bedroom."

"That's kind of my plan," she teased, flashing him a suggestive smile.

In one swift movement, Jack flipped her over, spreading her legs so the weight of his body nestled between them. He reached below the covers. "Are you sure you want more?"

"Yes. More." Her words were a sultry demand.

Jack always knew exactly what she needed, finding a rhythm that soon had her moaning as his fingers slipped over her.

Carrie shuddered in his arms. Jack was like an addiction, a slow-burning need that could not be extinguished. She shuddered with anticipation. Sex with him got better every time.

He stroked her clit, and she arched against him in response. He dipped his head to kiss her breasts, circling her taut nipples with his tongue. Moaning with pleasure, she cupped his head in her hands, pulling on his hair as he tugged them with his teeth.

"Now," she urged when she could take no more.

Jack complied, shifting his hips to meet hers as he thrust deep inside her. They rocked together and Carrie gasped, the heat of their union rushing through her entire body.

He kissed her mouth hard, plunging his tongue between her expectant lips. He slid his hands beneath her bottom, grasping her hips as he pulled her firmly against him.

Desperate to be closer, she clenched her muscles and ground against him, following the sweet rhythm of his movements. She trailed her fingernails up his back. In an instant, heat rose in her core and exploded within her. She called Jack's name as spasms rocked her body.

A moment later, Jack found his own release for the second time that night. They collapsed against each other.

He rolled over, trying to catch his breath. Carrie pushed her damp, tangled hair away from her eyes and placed her cheek to Jack's chest, showering it with grateful kisses. "Do you still want to go back to work?" She bit her lower lip to suppress a smile. "Or can we just keep doing this all night?"

He laughed, still out of breath. "Baby, I think you are going to be the death of me."

She laughed, too, completely sated yet energized. And starving. After two rounds in Jack's bedroom, she was hungry for the wonton soup waiting in the takeout bag downstairs.

He trailed his fingers across the curve of her hip. "Why don't you stay here and get some sleep? I'll be home in a few hours."

"No, I'd better go, too," Carrie said. She dropped a casual kiss on his lips before hopping out of bed. "I've still got things to do tonight. We need to eat, and then you can drop me off outside the hotel before going back to work."

****

Jack watched Carrie retreat into the bathroom, then swung his legs over the edge of the bed and sat up. In the stillness of the room, he could hear the thumping of his heart as his body drifted down from the high. How the hell did she have so much energy while he was still panting like he'd just run a race?

Even after more than a week, his mind reeled with disbelief. In his entire life, he had never been with a woman who one minute could be sharing a mind-blowing sexual experience, and the next laughing and teasing and getting dressed to go home. With Carrie, there was no pressure to define their relationship or talk about emotions or even spend the night together out of obligation. She didn't make demands or try to take advantage of his position, the way other women in his past had done.

If anything, she was all give and no take. Hell, she wouldn't even move into the damn villa he'd offered her. She didn't care about his money or what was in it for her. Being with her was just…easy.

On one hand, he should be grateful. Wasn't it every man's fantasy to have endless great sex with a beautiful woman, no strings attached?

Then instead of being happy, why was it bugging the hell out of him?

Since day one, Carrie had not minced words about her desire to keep their relationship a secret. But tonight, when she flashed him a lighthearted smile before closing the bathroom door, he realized she meant

152

it. For her, this affair was about sex and having fun and drinking in every ounce of an exciting new city. He had assumed, somewhere in the depths of his mind, she'd eventually come around, and they'd figure out a plan to make things work. But it was clear to him now. She had no interest in anything beyond their temporary agreement.

Ever since his conversation with Mark in the security office, Jack had put a lot of thought into what it was he was looking for in life. No longer was he content with being the big boss, spending every waking hour at work, surrounded by people who kissed his ass because he had something they all wanted. It was all so superficial and sordid. He was ready for more. He was ready for what his brother Doug had—a home, a wife, and children.

And now he realized, without a doubt, he wanted those things with *her*.

Jack sighed, opening the bathroom door to join Carrie in the shower. Too bad he also knew convincing her to stay in Las Vegas with him was about as safe a bet as hitting the jackpot on a slot machine two times in a row.

Chapter Eleven

The next morning dawned the day of Antonio Cardini's arrival. His private plane was due to land late in the afternoon, giving Carrie the better part of the day to finish preparations.

The restaurant was almost ready for the grand opening, with the kitchen stocked, menus printed, and final interior touches complete. She met with Sherry and Frank to finalize Antonio's itinerary for the days leading up to the restaurant's grand opening. Then she excused herself to go make follow-up calls to the journalists who had not yet committed to covering the grand opening.

Many of Las Vegas's biggest headliners and even a handful of celebrities had accepted their invitations to the press party. Jack hired extra security for the event. Between the hype of the celebrity guest list and anticipation for Antonio Cardini's newest restaurant, she had her work cut out making sure everything was organized and ready for the media. It was the biggest event of her career so far, and no matter what the outcome, one thing was certain. The next week of her life was shaping up to be a very busy one.

Carrie was finishing the salad she'd ordered for lunch from room service when her phone rang.

"Ready to go?" Jack's voice greeted her on the other end of the line. She had forgotten they'd made

154

plans to tour the hotel.

On the drive back to the hotel the night before, they'd been discussing work when Jack realized she had not yet been given an official grand tour. It was an excuse to spend time alone together during the day, Carrie realized, but nonetheless, a tour of the hotel would be beneficial if she planned to continue handling the Grand Portofino's PR after the opening of Cardini's.

With so much work still to get done, her first instinct was to tell him she was too busy. But the notion of an afternoon with Jack in his element was too much to resist. "Sure, I'll be right down."

Jack was leaning against the hotel's check-in counter when she arrived in the lobby, his elbow propped on the gleaming marble top, chatting with a young, pretty clerk. Even from a distance, Carrie felt the pull of his body, but she took a moment to observe him from afar.

His tall frame was angled to the side, giving her the perfect perspective to take in his handsome, chiseled profile. Even in the vast openness of the Grand Portofino's lobby, everything about him filled the space. His presence was compelling, with an air of authority that appeared effortless. Jack held himself in total confidence, his feet set apart the width of his broad shoulders and a dynamic smile illuminating his face. And damn, the man knew how to wear a suit.

The clerk giggled at whatever Jack said, and a flash of jealousy swept over her. She walked over to the pair, resisting the urge to wrap a possessive arm around Jack's waist. Instead, she announced her arrival with a professional smile and casual, "Sorry I'm a few minutes late."

"Miss Thomas. Hi," the girl said.

Carrie masked her surprise as Jack said, "Carrie, this is Kristen Lewis, one of our front desk managers."

"Hello." Carrie shook her outstretched hand.

"Mr. Dillon was just telling me about the big event this weekend for the new restaurant."

"Kristen's fiancé works for Frank in the food and beverage department," he said.

"Oh, how wonderful." Relief washed over her, and Carrie felt infinitely stupid for the unwelcome rush of insecurity. She had no right to be jealous, anyway. Jack was only hers for a couple of weeks.

As the three of them stood together making small talk, it was obvious now he only had eyes for her. In fact, he was staring at her a little too intently, considering they were in mixed company.

"We'd better get started on our tour, Mr. Dillon," she said, adopting her most professional tone. "Nice to meet you, Kristen."

She raised an eyebrow as they turned away from the front desk staff, and Jack shrugged. "You look hot," he said in way of explanation.

She laughed and shook her head. "You're incorrigible."

There wasn't much to see Carrie hadn't already stumbled across during her first two weeks in Las Vegas. He walked her through the hotel's front offices and several of the resort's establishments that were closed during the day, including the theater and the Grand Portofino's nightclub, the Riviera Room. With her busy schedule, she had not taken the time to experience either one.

Jack ticked off the names of entertainers scheduled to perform. The big names impressed her but not as much as the pride in his voice when he talked about them. The passion with which Jack ran his business inspired her.

They took an escalator to the resort's conference center. "Have you seen our wedding chapels yet?" Jack asked.

"No," Carrie said. "Sherry told me they were nice, but I haven't had the chance to check them out."

"We have two." He led her down an opulent corridor. Keeping with the Grand Portofino's elegant Mediterranean theme, the hotel's wedding area was awash with fragrant flowers, brilliant shades of blue, white, and terracotta, and a wall of massive arched windows that overlooked the resort's tropical pool area. "They're among the nicest in all of Las Vegas. If I had known they were going to be so popular, I would have had the architect put in three or four. The wedding chapels are booked solid for the next three months."

He opened an ornate wood door to reveal what Carrie thought was one of the loveliest rooms she had ever seen. The chapel was decorated in the same hues as the hallway, with rich mahogany furnishings. The sweet smell of flowers permeated the room.

"How beautiful," Carrie exclaimed. She leaned in to smell an arrangement of white lilies on a table just inside the doorway. "Oh, Jack, I had no idea. I always thought Vegas wedding chapels were either cheesy drive-through places or were run by middle-aged Elvis impersonators. But this is gorgeous."

"So are you," Jack said in a low voice. But he smiled, looking genuinely pleased to hear she liked the chapel. "We have professional wedding planners on staff and can accommodate ceremonies in just about any faith. It was very important to me to make sure every wedding at the Grand Portofino be refined and classy, and also a stress-free experience for the couple getting married."

"I can't imagine a more beautiful spot to get married," Carrie said in a wistful voice, following him into the corridor. Across the hall, an identical wedding chapel was filling with guests.

"I think a ceremony is about to start." He glanced at his watch. "Want to check it out?"

"Do you think anyone would mind?"

"I don't think so," he said, leading her into the chapel. They stood with some of the other wedding guests behind the last pew. The room was packed, and nobody noticed they were strangers to the couple.

After a few minutes, the crowd settled into place and an organist at the front of the chapel played the wedding march. Carrie joined the crowd in an audible gasp when she saw the beautiful bride begin her short walk down the aisle. She wore a strapless white wedding gown and glowed with happiness.

Carrie had never seen a smile so genuine as when the bride turned toward her betrothed. They beamed at each other as the minister spoke, and she prickled with envy witnessing the woman's unmistakable happiness.

The minister said a prayer. From the corner of her eye, she saw Jack turn her way but dared not look at him. His eyes burned into her. She listened to the couple exchange their wedding vows.

Carrie watched the couple gaze into each other's eyes as they spoke. The love between them was obvious, and all of a sudden, she felt betrayed by her own heart. The love these two strangers shared was deeper than anything she had ever experienced, and for the first time, she was one hundred percent confident in her decision to end her engagement to David. She never loved him the way a woman should love the man she is about to marry, not the way this bride loved her groom. She had never known such a love existed. Not this kind of love, one that made your skin glow, voice tear, and made forever sound like not long enough to share your life with another person.

Carrie did not know when Jack had taken her hand, but she realized he was holding it. She stared at their entwined fingers. His hand dwarfed hers. She felt safe and protected just holding it, and when he squeezed her hand, she could feel his strength. She squeezed him back.

The room was so still she could feel the pulse of his thumb on the top of her fingers. She held her breath and did her best to maintain a placid exterior, but her mind zoomed in circles.

Confusion overwhelmed her. Sure their hands were locked together now, but where would they be in a month? Two weeks had sounded like an adventure when they agreed to this plan in the beginning, but the more time she spent with him, the more she realized how hard it would be to say goodbye when it was all over. She didn't want a Vegas rendezvous; she wanted the real thing.

She wanted what this couple had.

And she wanted it with Jack.

But those things weren't in the cards for them. Carrie had too many goals to accomplish before she could set her own ambitions aside to be a wife. If she wanted to move ahead at Cresswell & Dailey, she needed to stay focused on her career and continue to keep this affair a secret. She wasn't about to blow all she had worked so hard to achieve just because a guy gave her multiple orgasms.

The tension between them had been mounting over the last couple of days. The sex was amazing, mind-blowing, one could even say. But the more time they spent together, the more she could feel Jack pulling her toward him. Their relationship was a tug of war, Jack pulling in one direction and her job in the other. Sooner or later, the rope was bound to snap.

From the front of the chapel, the minister declared, "I now pronounce you husband and wife."

The bride and groom kissed, and their friends and family broke into a round of applause. Carrie let go of Jack's hand, but she could not bring herself to join in the cheers. At last, she turned to meet his questioning gaze. The fire in his eyes implored her, demanding answers to the questions she wasn't ready to give. She followed him out of the chapel and into the empty corridor.

"Carrie." In one swift movement, Jack's arm flew around her waist, and he spun her body against the wall with so much force she heard the thump. She let out a soft moan as he pressed his body possessively into hers. He kissed her, hands sliding down her sides.

"Oh my God," she groaned, and he took the opportunity to plunge his tongue through her parted lips. His hungry mouth devoured hers, and she returned the kiss with equal zeal. She ran her fingers through his hair, tugging him closer. Her body was crushed between the wall and Jack's hard chest. It was intoxicating to be trapped under the weight of the man who ruled her every thought. Indeed, one day soon that rope might snap, but right now all she wanted was him.

Her body pressed to his, she felt the distinct vibration of his cell phone ringing. Without releasing her from their embrace, he reached into his pocket and fumbled to silence it.

"Let's go to your room," he said, lips still pressed to hers, his voice husky with need. He was breaking their number one rule of mixing business with pleasure, but for once she didn't care. Her desire to be with him burned through her with an insistence powerful as a hot summer storm. He pulled away from the kiss and their eyes met, full of longing and unspoken affection. She nodded in agreement.

But before they had the chance to move, the chapel door swung open, and the entire wedding party poured from the room. Jack leaped back, and she shimmied away from the wall. The crowd of people came between them, shattering the magic moment.

It took a few tries before he could push his way against the flow of people to rejoin her. But by then, she had regained her composure and smoothed her tousled hair. She was still dizzy with desire, but the interruption had allowed her a moment to find her senses.

"Do you think anyone saw us?" Carrie asked.

"Nobody in there knows who we are." He banished the notion.

"Are you kidding?" She glanced at the crowd of people making their way down the hall to the reception area. "The wedding coordinator works for you, and I know I've seen those guys hanging around the food and beverage office."

Jack followed her gaze to the young waiters passing out champagne outside of the banquet room. "I don't think we need to worry about them."

"Still." She straightened. "We need to be more careful when we're in public."

"Fine." His jaw set in annoyance.

Tears sprang to her eyes. She could tell he was frustrated, and she was too, but their frustration stemmed from different places. Jack made it clear he hated sneaking around, but he did it anyway for her. She hated that the world they lived in made sneaking around necessary in the first place.

Jack reached for her, but her gaze darted past him, and she pulled away from his reach. "What are you so afraid of?"

Her chin dropped to her chest, and the burning tears she'd been fighting to hold in won the battle. When she looked at him again, her cheeks were streaked with wetness. "If you have to ask, then you don't know me at all."

"I know you," he said, with a softness in his voice she had never heard.

He wiped the tears off her cheeks with the smooth pad of his index finger. "But I also know when you love somebody, you shouldn't be afraid of showing it. You shouldn't want to hide it from the people you know best. You should want to shout it out to the world."

Jack's cell phone rang again. His forehead wrinkled and with an exasperated sigh, he pulled it from his pocket and answered with a brusque, "Jack Dillon."

Carrie heard Frank Giotto's voice on the other end. "Where the hell are you? Antonio Cardini's limousine arrived twenty minutes ago. We've been waiting in the upstairs conference room."

"Be right there." He disconnected without another word. Turning to Carrie, his voice softened. "I'm sorry, I have to go. But we're not done talking about this, not by a long shot."

She nodded, unable to look at him. She didn't want him to see all the raw emotion she knew was plastered on her face.

His hand touched her face again. "I'll see you later?" It was not a question, though.

She nodded again, this time offering him her best shot at a reassuring smile. But it felt strained and flat on her face. He retreated to the end of the hall, his stride swift and assured, and disappeared down the escalator to the casino level.

Alone in the hallway, Carrie leaned against the wall for support, struggling to make heads or tails of what just transpired.

Had Jack told her he loved her?

Chapter Twelve

Confusion overwhelmed her. Carrie needed to talk to someone, and there was only one person she knew would understand.

"Hello?"

She leaned back in the yellow armchair in her suite, gripping the telephone as if it were a lifeline. "Phyllis, this is Carrie."

"Hey, rock star," Phyllis greeted her. "How are things in Las Vegas?"

Although she had planned to talk to Phyllis about the situation in a dignified manner, Carrie burst into tears. "Phyllis, I think I screwed up."

Twenty minutes later, the entire story was in the open. She was relieved to have finally shared her feelings with a friend and surprised Phyllis was not upset to learn about Carrie's relationship with their client.

"I know you do a hell of a job from nine to five," Phyllis said. "What happens in your personal life after-hours is nobody else's business."

Despite her boss's blessing, Carrie still couldn't help but feel wary about the situation. "What about Jim?"

"Jim would definitely *not* approve," Phyllis said. "But I'll make sure he doesn't find out. Besides, I wouldn't worry about him too much. The man's got his eye on retirement…and the sooner the better."

Carrie smiled through her tears. Though it was a long way off, the idea of Jim Cresswell leaving the company thrilled her to bits. He was just one part of the problem though. "I don't want Jack's staff to find out, either."

"So don't tell them," Phyllis said. "You said yourself so far nobody has found out. Sounds like you are being very discreet."

So far, Carrie thought. She stopped short of telling Phyllis about Jack's growing impatience. The memory of their fiery kiss against the wall outside the wedding chapel crashed over her. And his frustration when she pushed him away after the chapel doors opened and all those people rushed out. It was the closest they'd come to getting caught, and it gnawed at her knowing their indiscretions might someday soon come back to haunt them.

"It's just so frustrating."

"You know," Phyllis said, "there are worse things in life than being pursued by a handsome billionaire."

"You make it sound so fairytale-like." Carrie couldn't hide the bitterness in her voice. Jack's money was the last thing on her mind. "It's not that simple, Phyllis. Even if we were able to work things out with my job, there's still the tiny detail of *we live in different states*."

"Quit making excuses." Phyllis clucked her tongue. "You're afraid if you give in to your feelings, it wouldn't last anyway. You're afraid of losing your heart to a man who would always put his work before you, and you don't want to get hurt. I know you, Carrie Thomas."

She swallowed hard as Phyllis's words hit home. "We agreed it would only be for two weeks."

"Nonsense," the older woman exclaimed in her brash New York way. "If you two care about each other, you'll find a way to make the long-distance issue work."

"But he's a client, Phyllis. What happens if things go sour? How am I supposed to keep working on this account if we end up hating each other? I mean, we have to talk every day. And what about his employees? I don't want anyone to think Cresswell & Dailey got this account because of my relationship with Jack."

"You're a smart girl for being wary about mixing business with pleasure," Phyllis said. "As your boss, I respect your integrity. But as a woman, let me tell you. A successful career will only take you so far. Love...love is what matters."

"Excuse me?"

"Look at me," her boss confided. "I'm not getting any younger. I'm the president of a major PR firm, and what do I have to show for it? Money in the bank, a well-respected name in the industry? But who do I have to go home to every night? A cat. Now tell me if that isn't the most pathetic stereotype you've ever heard."

"I don't know what to say." Carrie was caught off guard by Phyllis's unexpected admission. She never thought of her boss as being lonely before. A bolt of guilt flashed over her for going on and on about Jack.

"Don't say anything, just listen." Phyllis's voice rang with conviction. "If you see the chance at love, you grab it. Life is too short to stand on ceremony."

Her words were still fresh in Carrie's mind as she waited for Jack to arrive that night. She had hoped the talk with Phyllis would set her straight back on her career path. Instead, she was more confused than ever.

Somewhere along the line, she had managed to convince herself if they kept their relationship on its two-week timeline, she'd be able to return to New York after and forget about her feelings for him. They could spend this time in Las Vegas having fun, making love, sneaking around like a pair of teenagers, but when their two weeks were up, she would return to her life, and Jack would move on with his.

Wrong.

What she hadn't counted on was how deeply he had crawled under her skin. Being with him had become as necessary as breathing. The thought of spending even one day without him by her side was frightening. How were they ever going to be able to say goodbye?

And they had to say goodbye, didn't they? Even if Phyllis was right, and nobody on Jack's team cared they were together, one fact remained. They lived on opposite ends of the country. Carrie was not about to sacrifice her career and move to Las Vegas just so she could be with a man.

She let out a long, painful breath. Maybe the best thing to do was end it now before they got in any deeper.

The telephone rang, interrupting her thoughts. She answered it with a shaky hand.

"Carrie, it's me." Jack's voice rose above the sound of a crowd in the background.

"Where are you?"

"Downstairs at Steak House. We took Antonio to dinner, and now I think we're heading out for a few drinks. I'm sorry, but I have to cancel our plans for tonight."

She was surprised to find herself relieved. At the unexpected reaction, she sat on the edge of her desk chair and swiveled it around. "It's all right." She forced her voice to be cheerful. Maybe it would be better if she didn't see him tonight. It would give her more time to think, to decide what she wanted to do.

"I can come by later…"

"No, don't come up."

"I don't think we'll be too late tonight." The disappointment in his voice was evident.

"Jack, I have to ask you something," Carrie said, wishing her voice was not so shaky. "What you said outside the wedding chapel…"

"What did I say?"

"I think you said you loved me." It was a statement, but it came out sounding more like an accusation.

The stunned silence on the other end of the line was all she needed to hear.

He cleared his throat. "Listen, whatever I said…did I say that?"

"Yes. I mean, I think so."

"You think so?"

"You said when you love somebody, you should shout it out to the world."

"Huh," Jack said. "I guess I did."

"So is that how you feel?" Carrie closed her eyes. It didn't matter if he answered yes or no. Either way, they were going down a dangerous path.

Another pause. Then, he lowered his voice even more and asked, "What if I said it was?"

"Then I'd say we should hang up and never speak again."

"Why?" Jack's tone gave way to exasperation. "Where is this coming from, Carrie?"

"You know where," she said. "We agreed to two weeks. If we start throwing around words like love, everything will get screwed up."

"We?" Jack challenged. "So then you feel the same way?"

"That's not what I said."

She heard him sigh, and then the buzz of voices in the background grew louder, reminding Carrie he was not alone. They must have reminded Jack, too. "Listen," he said. "Can we talk about this later? I've got Antonio and half a dozen other people waiting for me to get off my phone."

Carrie conceded. The last thing she wanted was for her colleagues to witness Jack having a lovers' spat on his cell phone.

"Can I call you later?" he asked.

"Tomorrow," she said. "Call me tomorrow."

****

Jack stepped onto the elevator from the lobby of the Grand Portofino and rode to his office on the thirtieth floor. It was late, and he didn't have any work to do that couldn't wait, but the thought of returning home alone made him sting with loneliness.

As he unlocked the suite and entered his dark office, he thought about his conversation with Carrie. *Did I really say I loved her?*

He couldn't remember if he'd said it or not, but thinking about it now, he realized it would have been the truth if he did. At least, the possibility of falling in love with her was there. It was a possibility Jack wanted to explore, and he wanted Carrie to do it with him. But they couldn't explore anything so long as she was being so bull-headed about cutting all ties when their two weeks were up. God, she drove him crazy.

Jack's past was speckled with other women—romances that never took off, gold diggers interested in him for his looks or his money, even the occasional one-night stand—but this was the first time in his life he had met somebody with whom he could honestly picture having a future.

He knew they had a lot of obstacles standing in their way, but he was a problem solver. And he was used to getting his way. There was no way in hell he wasn't going to find a solution to this problem.

Without turning on the light, he sank into the leather chair behind his glass desk and swiveled to look out the window. The Strip below glittered and danced with blinking lights. It was a view he loved, one that usually excited and motivated him to conquer the city. But tonight, he longed for the peaceful, star-lit calm of a desert night sky.

He turned in his chair and observed his office with a critical eye, thinking about what Carrie had said the week before in his living room. He wondered if she thought his office was as "showy" as his house. The room was decorated with steel-gray, glass furniture, and a black leather couch. But like his house, there were only the necessary furnishings in his oversized office. Nothing extra, no pictures on the wall or plants to add a little life to the room. Was this how people perceived him—cold and sleek and right to the point?

He decided to have Grace order a few palm trees

for his office in the morning.

Palm trees solved one problem. Now, what was he going to do about the woman who had taken over his every waking thought?

Cardini's grand opening day sped toward them, and then if she had her way, Carrie would be gone. He wasn't ready to accept that reality.

Jack stared at the lights of the Strip for a long time, thinking about Carrie and wondering what he could do to convince her to stay with him in Las Vegas. It did not take him long to come up with a plan.

Chapter Thirteen

Carrie opened the door to her suite the next evening to find Jack leaning against the door frame. As usual, the first sight of him took her breath away. He wore jeans and an untucked button-down shirt, a pair of sunglasses hanging casually from the top pocket. He must have changed in his office upstairs because just an hour ago, he'd been at a meeting dressed in a power suit. He pulled off both looks with equal perfection.

"Hope I'm not late." Stepping inside, he dropped a kiss on her cheek.

It had taken a lot of convincing, but when Jack promised a romantic dinner to make up for missing the night before, she agreed to see him. They only had a few nights left before her return to New York, and she didn't want to ruin them with pointless talk about the future.

But he wasn't dressed for a romantic dinner. Carrie swept her gaze over his casual outfit. "Where are we headed tonight?"

"It's a surprise," Jack said, his gaze on her as she closed her laptop.

"Let me go change." She started for the bedroom, but Jack caught her by the wrist, swinging her back around into his arms.

"You look great." He planted a kiss on her lips.

She laughed at the unexpected kiss. "But I'm

wearing jeans."

"Me too." Jack steered her toward the door. She grabbed her purse off the table. "Trust me. Where we're going, jeans are perfect."

Driving off from the valet stand in front of the hotel, Carrie was surprised to see Jack make a left onto Las Vegas Boulevard instead of a right. She expected him to drive into town to one of the restaurants he was always talking about taking her to check out. Instead, he drove away from the lights of the Strip, onto the highway, and into the calm of the desert.

It was already dark out, and she peered at the sky through the moon roof of Jack's Audi. "It's a beautiful night."

"Uh-huh." He kept his eyes on the road.

"So where are we going?" Carrie possessed all the patience of a ten-year-old.

Jack burst out laughing. "If I told you, it wouldn't be a surprise."

She gazed through the window for a long time. The Mojave Desert surrounded them, a vast expanse of open land marked by cacti, rocks, and bramble bushes that rose from the arid landscape. "We're in the middle of nowhere."

"That's the point." He pulled off the highway and drove down a narrow sandy road. About a hundred feet from the main road, he stopped the car and got out. The slam of his door echoed in the open desert.

Carrie followed. "What is this place?"

"It's the desert, silly." He flashed her a smile. As Carrie looked around their desolate surroundings, Jack opened the trunk and removed a wicker picnic basket and a large Mexican blanket.

She gasped when she realized what he was doing. "Oh my God, I can't believe you went through all this trouble." She rushed to his side and helped him lay the blanket across the rocky ground.

"You said you wanted to go somewhere where nobody would recognize us." Jack set the picnic basket on the blanket. The look he gave her was raw and sincere. "I think we'll be pretty safe here."

A warm glow rushed through her. Every time she thought she had Jack Dillon pegged, he did something wonderful to change her view of him. They sat on the blanket, and Jack opened the picnic basket, removing the contents and placing them on the blanket one by one. "Roasted chicken, potato salad, fresh fruit, a bottle of vino, and last but not least…" He removed a single long-stem red rose from the basket. "For you."

"Thank you, Jack," she said, leaning over the basket to kiss him. She took a long smell of the rose, then set it across the top of the basket where she'd be able to see it all night.

He poured the wine into two glasses and handed one to her.

"Shall we make a toast?" she asked.

"If you like."

She raised her glass, remembering the first time they had toasted together at Steak House. It seemed like a lifetime ago. "To fate."

"Are you finally admitting serendipity has played a role in all that has happened since you got here?" Jack's eyes twinkled.

She smiled, not giving him the satisfaction of an answer. Jack set his wineglass on top of the picnic basket without clinking it to hers.

174

The smile fell from her face. "What's wrong?"

"I don't like that toast, after all."

"Why not?"

He touched her hair. "Because as much as I believe it was fate that brought us together, I also believe whatever happens next is in our own hands."

She stared at him. "We know what happens next, Jack. My time in Las Vegas will be up, and then I'll go back to New York." *Like Cinderella's carriage turning into a pumpkin at midnight. Her ball gown turning into rags.* Carrie shuddered at the metaphors that popped into her head.

He studied her, his eyes pensive and brimming with some indefinable emotion. "I made a big mistake thinking we'd be able to have these two weeks together and then just say goodbye. I wasn't counting on falling in love with you."

His unexpected admission sent her heart plummeting into the pit of her stomach. Speechless, she allowed Jack to continue.

"We've been very naïve, Carrie, thinking we could get away with this plan of ours. When I watched that couple getting married yesterday, I knew without a doubt I wanted to have what they have." As if to make absolutely sure she got the point, he added, "With you."

Carrie shook her head. "Are you asking…"

"No. I'm simply saying don't go home, Carrie. Stay with me in Las Vegas and give us a real chance."

She braced her hands against the Mexican blanket to keep from falling over. This was not supposed to happen. This was not supposed to be the end result of their time together. They were supposed to enjoy each other's company, have all the great sex they could handle, and then say goodbye. There was not supposed to be talk of love and commitment and moving across the country.

"I can't, Jack." Her head was spinning. "We had a deal."

"I want to make a new deal."

It was useless to rationalize with a man who lived and breathed business deals every day of his life. But she was not a piece of investment real estate he could take control of on a whim.

"What about my job?" she asked. "Do you expect me to throw away everything I've worked so hard to accomplish to move here with you?"

"Of course I don't," Jack said. "I have a proposition for you."

She raised an eyebrow. "A proposition?"

"Yes." He took a long sip of wine. "A business proposition. I've been discussing it with Sherry and some of the hotel's advisors, and we've decided it may be more practical to hire a full-time Director of Public Relations rather than keep an agency on retainer."

"And I suppose you see me as this full-time PR Director?"

"As a matter of fact, yes. You'd start working at the Grand Portofino, then in time move on to do publicity for my other hotels, as well." Seeing the skepticism in Carrie's expression, he added, "It's a great opportunity for you."

"Why me?"

"Because I've seen your work, and it's impressed me. I think you'd be a strong player for my team." He refilled his wineglass. "You're the only person I'd want for the job."

"Bullshit," Carrie laughed. "You just want me out here to be with you."

He took a sip and flashed her a guilty smile. "Well, isn't that the point? I thought so hard to find a way for us to be together, and I think this could work. You told me from the start you wanted to keep our relationship a secret from Jim Cresswell. And I've respected your wishes. But work for me and there won't have to be any more secrets."

No more secrets. It did sound tempting, but she wasn't convinced. "I'd still be working for you. It doesn't feel right."

"There's more to it," he said. "I'm looking at building another new property in Las Vegas. I need a PR person who knows the ins and outs of this town. Cresswell & Dailey is a great agency, but they're based in New York. I need someone local, and there are no agencies in Nevada good enough for the job. It's the reason I hired you in the first place, Carrie. I wouldn't offer this job to you if I didn't think it was the best move for my company."

"So this is your solution?" she challenged. "Move me to Vegas? What about my friends? My parents? My life in New York? Why am I the one who must give up everything, and you don't have to give up anything?"

Jack raised a hand to silence her barrage of questions. "With the money you'll be making, you can fly to New York every weekend if you want." He told her the salary the Grand Portofino was prepared to offer. Carrie's eyes widened. The proposed number was almost double what she was making now at Cresswell & Dailey.

"It's not charity, either," he said. "It's the going

rate for a Public Relations Director at a major resort. I had Sherry research it for me."

"What else?" Jack's offer was tempting, but she was not about to sell out just to please a man. Time to play hardball.

"You'll have your own office at the hotel, and we'll pay for you to relocate to Las Vegas, of course. Whenever you're ready."

"Oh, Jack, I don't know. I need to think about all this."

"What's there to think about?"

"Well, Phyllis for one thing." Carrie's brow wrinkled. "She's been very good to me, and I feel like I'd be betraying her. If you pulled the account from Cresswell & Dailey and hired me full time, it would be a real loss for the agency."

"We'd honor the contract, Carrie," he said. "And then just not renew it. People do it all the time. It's business."

"It's not just business when friends are involved."

"I respect your loyalty," Jack said. He bit into one of the strawberries from the picnic basket and continued to talk with his mouth full. "But she'll understand what a tremendous opportunity this is for you. If she's the friend and mentor you think she is, Phyllis will be supportive."

She fidgeted with the rose, thinking about what Phyllis had said the day before. Jack was right; after the way Phyllis had preached to her about grabbing hold of a chance at love, she would understand.

She wanted to accept his offer. All of it. It sounded like paradise, their love in the open for the entire world to see, and a job she knew she had earned and deserved.

Since the night they met, Carrie knew in her bones Jack was the one for her. What a fool she had been to pretend they could pull off this game of nothing-but-sex and then walk away unscathed. She had loved him from the start.

Another obstacle occurred to her. "I don't want people to think the reason I got my job was because…"

"We won't tell anybody until after the big press event," he said. "Besides, everybody here has tremendous respect for you. People will think you got the job because you are smart and hardworking and good for the business." He picked up another strawberry and pointed at her with it. "Which, by the way, is one hundred percent true."

"Really?"

"Yes, really." He popped the fruit in his mouth.

"But do you think it could work, Jack?" she asked, finally allowing those petals of excitement to burst into full bloom. "You as my boss, and us a couple at the same time?"

"Baby, just trust me." Jack took her hand in his. "Ever since the night Mark went into the hospital, I've come to realize life is too short to take things for granted. We've got something special happening between us. I don't want to lose you."

Carrie's heart was racing. She hated making rush decisions. But studying their entwined fingers, only one answer made any kind of sense. He gave her hand a squeeze, and that simple gesture solidified her decision. For once, she allowed her heart to rule her head. "I'll do it."

"You will?"

"Yes." Her face broke into a wide grin. "I will."

Jack pulled her close and kissed her. His mouth tasted sweet from the strawberries and wine. With Carrie still in his arms, he fell back on the blanket and rolled over, pinning her beneath him. Their legs were tangled in a heap, and she was pretty sure they had knocked over the dish of potato salad.

"I usually seal business deals with a handshake," he said, lowering his lips again to hers. "But I think tonight this may be more appropriate."

She returned his kiss with eager abandon, certain she must be dreaming.

After a minute, Jack broke the kiss. He raised his head and looked at her with a playful grin. "I have one more proposition for you."

Carrie gazed at him, his face framed by the velvet black sky and millions of stars twinkling above. Never before had she seen such a perfect night sky. "What's your proposition?"

"I bet you've never made love outside in the desert before."

Carrie gave him a coy smile. "I've never made love outside anywhere before."

"Oh, my darling." His hands inched their way up her tee shirt. "You've got a lot to learn about the great outdoors."

Chapter Fourteen

Carrie rushed through an Instagram post she was writing for the resort, eager to put the workday behind her and spend time with Jack. Anticipation flowed through her like a river, but she wouldn't be able to relax until she had all her loose ends wrapped up.

"Want to go see a concert tonight?" Jack entered the suite and crossed the room to where she was working. She had given him his own key card, a natural next step in their relationship, which had been on fast forward since day one.

"Hang on a second..." Carrie said, not looking at him. All week long she'd been hard at work, barely coming up for air. They were just a few days away from the big event.

"I'm sorry. What did you say?" She saved her draft and turned to face him.

"Concert. Tonight."

"Oh, I don't know," she said. The prospect of running into anyone they knew left her uneasy. "I thought we were still keeping our relationship quiet until after the press event on Saturday?"

"There's a cool old-school band playing at a casino in Henderson," Jack suggested. "It's only fifteen minutes away from the Strip, and nobody will recognize us. I promise."

Though staying with him in the suite all night

appealed to her far more than going to a concert, she agreed. "Okay." She stopped to give him a long, languid kiss, then headed into the bedroom to change.

Jack followed her, scrolling through his phone as she slipped into jeans and a glittery top. She smirked. He was always multitasking.

"I'm almost ready," she said. Jack looked up from his phone, and his eyes grazed over her with approval. She slipped her feet into a pair of black heels. "I just want to stop by your office and grab something before we go. Grace called to tell me a messenger delivered a package for me this afternoon, and I want to see what it is."

He glanced at his watch. "It's past seven. If we don't leave right now, we'll miss the beginning of the show."

"It'll only take a second." Carrie headed toward the door. "My contact at Las Vegas Food & Wine said they were sending over an advance print copy of their next issue featuring Cardini's, and I want to see if this is it."

"The workday is over." He pulled her in for a kiss and squeezed her ass. "And if I don't get you out of this hotel this minute, I'm going to end up pulling these jeans right back off."

"That doesn't sound like the worst idea," she mused, her arms snaking around him. *And then when we're done, I can go upstairs and get the damn package.*

"Nope, I promised you two weeks of Vegas fun, and tonight we're going to a rock concert," Jack said. "Besides, you're the one always telling me not to work so hard, so now I'm telling you. Let's go have a good time and forget about work for a few hours. The package will still be there in the morning."

She considered his words. It wasn't like her to call it a day with business left unfinished, and it wasn't like him, either. But she supposed he was right. Work had ruled their entire week, and a night out would be a good release.

"Okay," she agreed, though against her better judgment. "Let's go."

But though she tried, Carrie couldn't shake the nagging feeling following her around all evening. They arrived as the concert started, taking their seats amidst the raucous audience. The theater pulsed with lights, cheers, and music so loud, her chair vibrated with the beat. She did her best to focus on having fun, and while she loved listening to '80s music and drinking beer, almost as much as she loved rocking out with Jack in the dark theater, her mind refused to get lost in the music.

The package was bothering her. What if it was important? What if it was something she needed to respond to before the end of the day? What if it was the magazine? She needed to read the article right away and pass it along to Antonio and her boss. *Las Vegas Food & Wine* was one of the most prestigious publications in the region.

Something else was bothering her, too. She didn't like the way Jack had ordered her to stop working. Just because he wanted to make it to the concert on time, was she required to do as told? She hated being bossed around. It reminded her of the way David used to always call the shots, like a peacock fanning his feathers and expecting her to waddle obediently behind. And anything that reminded her of her ex-fiancé couldn't be good.

She fidgeted in her seat as the band shifted into a mellow metal ballad. Was this how it would be once she left Cresswell & Dailey and started working directly for Jack? The idea was unacceptable. She needed to be independent and in control of her own decisions and responsibilities. It was one thing to work with him as a client, but to have him as her actual boss was a whole other can of worms.

Carrie stole a glance at his profile in the dark theater. She didn't know why all of a sudden she was having second thoughts about accepting his job offer. Of course, she wanted to be with him—she was head over freaking heels for him—and the Director of Public Relations job was a dream come true. But had she jumped from the pot into the fire, rushing into a situation she was going to regret?

Stifling a sigh, she took a sip of beer from the plastic cup wedged between them in the seat's cup holder. Swallowing, she grimaced. The beer had grown warm and sour, just like her mood.

Since it was closer to drive to Jack's house after the concert rather than the hotel, they spent the night there. Carrie wanted to return to the Grand Portofino so she could run upstairs and grab the package, but after two beers and a long, tiring day, she didn't have the heart to ask Jack to make the drive. She would have to retrieve it before their staff meeting in the morning.

They drove back to the hotel together in the morning, slipping in a few minutes apart. Carrie went to her suite and took a long shower, wishing she could reclaim the complete happiness of a few days ago.

The uneasiness was unnerving. Between the

pressures of her job, the upcoming press event, and her reservations about working for Jack, second thoughts about their arrangement were mounting faster than ice cream melting in the hot Las Vegas sun.

She arrived on the thirtieth floor just as people were filing into the conference room for their staff meeting. She was disappointed to see Jack's assistant absent from her desk in the reception area. She went over to Grace's inbox and, finding it empty, slid behind the desk to see if she had slipped the package into one of the drawers.

"Hey, Carrie," Sherry greeted her from the other side of the desk, a puzzled expression on her face. "What are you doing?"

"Looking for a package Grace said arrived for me yesterday."

"Oh, Grace called in sick this morning," Sherry said, balancing her cup of coffee in one hand and a stack of papers on the other. "The meeting is about to start. Come on, I'll help you look for it later."

****

Jack sat alone in his office, catching up on email and getting his notes together for the morning meeting. Why was Grace always out sick on the days he needed her most? Today, he felt especially disorganized, and the two beers he had sucked down at the concert last night, coupled with two hours of heavy metal music and only two hours of sleep, added to his headache and inability to focus.

A thick yellow envelope caught his attention. There was a note from Grace attached, asking him to pass it on to Carrie.

The envelope wasn't sealed, so he peeked inside,

and seeing it was a magazine, slid it out to take a look. A brief note from the editor of *Las Vegas Food & Wine* was clipped to a feature article in the center of the magazine. He flipped it open and read the headline of the impressive two-page spread. "Chef Antonio Cardini Expands Restaurant Empire with Another Opening in Las Vegas."

He scanned the article, smiling as he read the very positive things the writer had said about both his hotel and Cardini's. Carrie would be very pleased.

"Jack." Sherry poked her head in the doorway and offered him a warm smile. "Everyone's in the conference room. Antonio, too. We're ready to begin whenever you are."

"Be right there." Jack slipped the magazine back into the envelope and shoved it into the pile of papers he was taking into the conference room. He would give it to Carrie after the meeting.

****

Since the day Antonio arrived in Las Vegas, Carrie had been working with him to prepare for the press event. But this staff meeting was her first opportunity to see him in a group setting with all the Grand Portofino's leaders. After they had finished discussing business, Antonio entertained the group with tales of his life in New York and Rome. He had a thick Italian accent and spoke with a booming voice. She knew right away he would be a big hit with the press at their grand opening event.

From across the conference room table, Antonio turned his attention to her. "You're from a big city, Carrie. I'm sure you must have interesting stories to share with us, too."

"I'm afraid nothing quite as exciting as the adventures you've had," she said. Although he was only in his forties, Antonio's culinary talents had led him around the globe, starring on TV shows and into the homes of movie stars and royalty.

"Don't be shy," Antonio said. "I'm sure a successful PR girl like you has had many adventures in New York."

Before Carrie could even protest the dreaded 'PR girl' term, Antonio snapped his fingers and said, "My goodness, I almost forgot. Speaking of PR girl, my assistant emailed me a copy of the *Las Vegas Food & Wine* article. The editor sent us an advance copy. *Tesoro!*"

"Oh, I..."

Antonio pulled a copy of the magazine from his leather folder. "Of course you've seen this, yes? She said they sent you a copy too. Fantastic job. You must have told the writer many great things for such a raving good article."

Feeling every set of eyes in the room lock on her, Carrie panicked for something to say. She knew with all her heart the missing package was a copy of that magazine.

Damn it, Jack! Why hadn't she insisted on going to the office last night to retrieve it? She felt like an incompetent fool, caught off guard by Antonio in front of Jack and all his staff.

"Tell me," Antonio asked. "What did you think of how the writer described all the new menu items?"

Carrie took a deep breath and summoned her most businesslike voice. "I think the article is great publicity for the restaurant." Her pulse pounded as she bluffed her way through the interrogation, hoping he wouldn't smell the bullshit. "I'm sure—"

"It was a great article, wasn't it?" Jack jumped in. He ignored the look of surprise Carrie shot him and smiled his most charming smile. "I made sure to get a copy right away. I like the part where they talked about your start in Florence, Antonio. You have such an impressive background."

"*Grazi*," Antonio said. "I am very glad to see you take such an active role in the PR for your hotel. I wouldn't have expected you to have seen the article yet, Jack."

Maneuvering the conversation like the expert salesman he was, Jack said, "Well, I have a great team, but I try to stay involved in all aspects of my hotel's operations."

Antonio smiled and turned to Carrie. "You are very lucky to be working with such an involved and intelligent client."

Involved and intelligent, my ass. She seethed. How dare Jack steal her thunder. She glared at him across the table. And where did he get a copy of the article, anyway?

Sherry glanced at her watch. "Oh my, it's almost ten o'clock already. Sorry to cut it short, but I have a conference call in a few minutes."

"We'd better get going, too," Frank said, standing. "Antonio and I have a meeting with the restaurant staff."

Within a few moments, the conference room cleared. Carrie waited for the door to close behind the last of her colleagues before turning to Jack with fiery eyes. "I cannot believe you just did that."

"What?" It was obvious he had no idea what she was so upset about, and his obliviousness enflamed her even more. Could he seriously not understand why this was a big deal?

"You deliberately interrupted me in front of Antonio and made me look inept." Her accusing eyes riveted on him.

"All I did was tell him the article was great. I knew you hadn't seen it, so I jumped in to help." He shrugged. "Is that so wrong?"

"Yes," she exclaimed. "Especially since I would have known about the article if you had just let me go get it last night like I wanted to, instead of rushing me off to make that stupid concert."

"Hey." Jack pointed at her. "You're the one who said you wanted to experience all Vegas had to offer."

"Well, I didn't know 'washed-up 80s hair band' would be on the list."

"Don't knock the band, Carrie," he warned, his expression so serious Carrie would have laughed if she wasn't so damn mad. "That music got me through high school in Toledo."

An image of teenage Jack in his bedroom listening to heavy metal crashed into her mind. She could totally see it.

"Besides," he reminded her, "you said you didn't want to bump into anyone we know. A-list bands don't play off the Strip."

With a sigh, she returned their conversation to the matter at hand. "Where did you get the article, anyway?"

"Grace left it for me to give to you." Jack shuffled through his papers and handed her the magazine.

"Here."

She took it from him. "You made me look stupid in front of a client, Jack. You made it look like I had no idea what I was talking about. Antonio looks to me to be on top of things when it comes to this PR campaign, and you undermined me."

"I don't think Antonio thought you looked stupid." Jack furrowed his brow. "I doubt he even realized you haven't read the article."

"Well, you made me *feel* stupid," she said, her voice weary. Why didn't he understand how important it was for her to always be on top of her game? Phyllis would have never put her in such an awkward position.

"Carrie," Jack said, "you work for me, not Antonio. Who cares what he thinks?"

"I care!" Fire rose in her chest. "Is this how it's going to be if I leave Cresswell & Dailey and come work for you? You thinking you have the right to jump in and take control of things? For your information, I was doing fine on my own."

"I was just trying to help."

"No, you were trying to rescue me. Just like at the Bellagio when that jerk in the bar was hitting on me. I am perfectly capable of taking care of myself. I don't need you to speak for me, especially when it comes to my business."

"It's *my* business we are talking about," Jack snapped. His face turned ashen. The mistake registered for him as fast as it had for Carrie. But it was too late to take it back. An awkward, heavy silence settled on the room.

"Then perhaps you should find somebody else to handle PR for *your* business," she said at last.

"Somebody who doesn't mind being treated like an incompetent idiot in front of other people."

He shook his head in disbelief. "You are making way too big a deal of this."

"Am I?" She lifted her chin. "All I ever asked was for one thing, Jack. One little thing. That we don't let our relationship interfere with my career."

"And you think it has?"

"Of course it has." Her voice rose in exasperation. "Would you have done the same thing if Antonio were talking to Sherry? Or Frank? And more importantly, last night, when I told you I wanted to go get my package, why didn't you just let me do it?"

"I don't have to justify myself to you." Jack crossed his arms. "This is my hotel, damn it."

And there it was. Carrie looked him straight in the eye, acutely aware of what she now had to do. "That's the problem, Jack. Because as my boss, you're right; you don't have to justify yourself." She swallowed hard. "But as my lover, you do."

Jack reached for her, but she stepped back. "I can't take this job, Jack. There's no way this will work if I do."

"Carrie, you're being unreasonable."

She closed her eyes, willing herself to stay strong. Why did he keep saying all the wrong things?

When she didn't respond, he asked, "So what about us? Are you turning down the job or turning down me, too?" His voice was low and wounded.

Carrie remained silent, unsure what to say, and fighting the tears threatening to escape from behind her closed eyelids.

"I suppose if you don't take the job, you'll go back

to New York after the press event Saturday night."

She sank into her chair at the conference room table. "Yes, I suppose I'd have to."

Jack nodded, a somber expression darkening his face. "So this is it? You're calling it quits on everything?"

Carrie's head throbbed. She knew what would happen if they attempted to keep things going. Nothing. With their hectic schedules, a long-distance relationship was not an option. And even if it was, there would still be the matter of keeping it secret from Jim Cresswell and the rest of their colleagues. It would never work.

"Well," she said, struggling to find the right answer, "we don't have to end it all. There are still a few days left before I leave. We can always go back to Plan A." But the words sounded hollow, even to her.

"You mean just fucking until you head home to New York?" Cold laughter rumbled off his lips. "No, thank you. I'm not that shallow."

His words cut through her like a blunt, bloody knife. A fresh rush of tears sprang to her eyes.

Seeing her injured expression, Jack said, "I'm sorry. I care about you too much to go back to that charade." He ran a gentle hand over the curve of her cheek. "We both know this has become more than just sex."

He was right. After everything they had said and done, if it wasn't going to be something real, something strong enough to last, what was the point?

When he spoke again, Jack's voice was strained and tight. "I can't go back to the way things were, not now. I respect your need to put your career first, but if that's the way you want it to be, then I think it would be best for us not to see each other at all anymore."

"So those are our options? All or nothing?" For a day that had started with such promise, it was now plummeting horribly out of control. She had awoken in the arms of this beautiful man and made love to him just hours ago. Used his toothbrush. Brewed coffee in his kitchen. How could they now be in this unthinkable place?

The room echoed in silence for a long moment, tension hanging between them. Then he answered, "Yeah, I guess so."

Carrie rose, anger and sadness and humiliation churning together in a kaleidoscope of raw emotion. She had never felt so rejected in her entire life. For a long moment, they stood staring at each other in silence. Then, she raised her chin and strode from the room.

She managed to keep the tears at bay until she was safely alone in the elevator. As the doors slid closed, she let them go like a damn bursting in a storm.

Chapter Fifteen

The sun was sinking behind the mountains as Jack drove home, taking with it the oppressive heat that had pounded Las Vegas all afternoon. He loosened his tie and turned the air-conditioning up a notch.

Two days had passed since he and Carrie ended things, and she was still avoiding him. Actually, "avoiding" was the wrong word. Avoidance would be easy. Avoidance would mean he wouldn't have to see her every day. Watch her marching around in those sexy little suits. Sitting through meetings in the same room. Pretending nothing had ever happened between them. Pretending he didn't have feelings for her when those very feelings dominated his every thought.

He'd ended things with plenty of women before, but never one he cared so much about. And not one he still had to see. In the past when a relationship ended, it was because the woman was getting too clingy, or demanding too much or sending off vibes she was after his money. Carrie did none of those things. In fact, with her, it was the opposite; the more he tried to give, the more she pushed him away. And the unfamiliar ground left him questioning everything.

It had taken a lot not to stop her when she walked out of the conference room. Maybe it was his stupid pride, but he couldn't bring himself to admit he was wrong about how things went down with that damn magazine article. Seeing Carrie standing there with a stony expression and accusing eyes left him too upset to speak at all.

He wasn't sure who he was even mad at, but instead of figuring it out, he did what had always worked for him in the past. Thrown himself into work. Without Carrie to spend time with, it was easy to get lost in the responsibilities of running his hotels.

But the things that used to excite him now felt endlessly grueling. Phone calls with his investors, operational issues, meetings, and now getting ready for this big press event for Cardini's. Where he used to find solace and satisfaction, work now left him discontent. Like something was missing he couldn't quite put his finger on, and he couldn't recapture it for all the money in the world.

And having Carrie still there to distract him made everything worse.

Jack sighed as he waited for the gates to open and turned into his development. With the opening of Cardini's approaching, it was impossible not to see her every day. Phyllis Dailey would be arriving from New York soon, and Carrie was determined to have all the details finalized before then. Even though he was paying the price, Jack had to respect the woman's grit and desire to impress her boss. After all, she had always been upfront in proclaiming her job was her priority, even during that blissful stretch of time when things were good between them.

The most ironic part was, despite his attraction to her in the beginning, he'd been resolved to let the whole thing go.

Then that damn slot machine hit the jackpot.

They'd been tempting fate from the moment they met, but he'd been a fool to credit the jackpot to fate. He shouldn't have taken it for anything more than the blind luck it was. And he definitely shouldn't have fallen for her.

One thing he knew now for sure. If he couldn't be with Carrie, he couldn't have her at his hotel distracting him. If she was making the decision to choose her career over him, then he owed it to the Grand Portofino to do the same.

"Oh, hell," Jack muttered, pulling into his driveway. When had life gotten so complicated?

****

The pool area of the Grand Portofino was a true desert oasis, with its abundant palm trees and sparkling water the same azure color of the sky. Taking a much-needed break from work, Carrie set her straw beach bag on one of the soft padded lounge chairs and stripped to her white swimsuit.

Ever since she ended things with Jack, Carrie felt the weight of her loss crushing her soul. And being here in Las Vegas was only making it worse. How could she get over him when she had to see him every day, live in his hotel, sleep in the bed they had made love on too many times to recall? She yearned to go home but leaving before the event this weekend was not an option.

She hoped a little time in the sun would help clear her mind. In one graceful move, Carrie eased into the pool, enjoying the sensation of cool water lapping against her skin. She dipped her head back to wet her hair and relaxed against the wall of the deep end.

The afternoon sun beat down, but since it was a

weekday, the pool was uncrowded. She swam to the other end and back, then hoisted herself out of the pool, her blonde hair slick against her scalp.

She returned to the lounge chair and slipped on her sunglasses. Spending time at the pool was the one thing in Vegas she'd miss for sure. She stretched on the chair and closed her eyes, enjoying the sun as it caressed her damp skin.

She did not see Jack approach until he was standing over her, blocking the sun's rays with his broad frame and casting a shadow over her body. She opened her eyes and gasped in surprise. He looked ridiculously out of place standing poolside in a charcoal-gray suit. A pair of aviator sunglasses masked the top half of his perfectly chiseled face.

He lowered himself onto the lounge chair beside hers.

"Hi." His voice was casual but held a pensive waver.

Carrie swung her legs to the ground and sat straight on the lounge chair, pulling a towel protectively around her shoulders. She wished she wasn't still so damned attracted to him. "Hello."

"Beautiful day, huh?"

She nodded. Had Jack really come to the pool wearing a suit and tie to talk about the weather? She looked at him, waiting, but was only met with her own reflection in the lenses of his sunglasses.

He cleared his throat. "I've been thinking about it, and as long as Phyllis Dailey is coming to Las Vegas for the Cardini's grand opening, there's no reason for you to stay, too. I'm sure you have a lot to catch up on in New York."

Caught off guard by Jack's unexpected statement, Carrie's eyes widened under her sunglasses.

"I think it would be best for both of us if you left the hotel."

"No," she told him. Who did he think he was, ordering her to stay in Las Vegas against her will when she first arrived and now ordering her to leave just because things between them had not worked out the way he wanted?

"No?" It was a word Jack was obviously unaccustomed to hearing.

"Hell no. I have too many balls in the air. If you want this restaurant opening to be a success, I need to be here to make it happen."

His jaw clenched. "I think Phyllis and Sherry will be able to handle things on this end."

"No way." Carrie shook her head. "It's my project, and I'm going to see it through."

They stared at each other for a long moment, their two pairs of sunglasses creating a wall between them. She was glad he could not see the tears of frustration welling in her eyes.

When she did not back down from their virtual staring contest, Jack rose from the edge of the lounge chair he was perched upon. "Well, do me a favor then and stop coming to my staff meetings every morning. I think your time here would be better spent working on the PR campaign."

He turned to leave, but Carrie called after him. "You asked me to attend those meetings, or did you forget?"

"Just do what you're here to do," he said, his face the color of the stone white pillars adorning the pool area. "My staff meetings are of no concern to you."

He walked toward the hotel, and Carrie fought hard to resist the urge to hurl her bottle of sunscreen at him. Instead, she rose and marched to the deep end, diving in headfirst without pause.

Taking long strokes, she swam across the pool in a fruitless attempt to clear her head of what had just transpired, but it was no use. She could be tenacious, but Jack was downright infuriating. She wanted to hit him. She wanted to quit. But she couldn't hit him, and she wouldn't quit. All she could do was swim.

****

It wasn't until later in the evening when she spoke to Phyllis on the phone, the tension that had settled on her heart like a heavy stone finally began to ease.

"I can't believe how callous he sounded," she said after describing the encounter. "It was like everything that happened between us never existed."

"He's in love with you."

"He told me to go back to New York." Carrie rolled her eyes as her temper flared again. She smoothed her hair over her shoulder. "Jack knows damn well this is where I belong right now."

"Then stay out of each other's way and get the job done," Phyllis instructed with a sigh. "We can talk more when I get into town tomorrow. Are you picking me up at the airport?"

"Yes." Carrie jotted down the flight information Phyllis read to her. "The hotel is sending a limo, and I will be there when we pick you up."

"I've asked Megan Summers to come to help with the event," Phyllis said. Megan was a junior account executive. She had just started working at Cresswell &

Dailey a few months earlier. "I figured we could use the extra help, and it will be good experience for her working a big event."

"Sure," Carrie agreed. The idea that Phyllis thought she couldn't handle it on her own ruffled her, but she dismissed the notion. Megan was young, smart, and motivated and would be a valuable extra set of hands the night of Cardini's grand opening. It would be good to have her there.

"She's not flying in until the day before, though, so it'll be just me at the airport tomorrow," Phyllis said.

After their call ended, Carrie let her gaze wander out the window to the Las Vegas Strip below. The view, once so enticing, tonight felt cold and lonesome. She'd been thinking about taking a walk and grabbing something to eat but instead crawled into bed and pulled the covers over her head, stifling the flashing lights of the Strip below. Maybe she'd order room service later. Or maybe she'd just go to sleep and skip dinner; she had no appetite anyway. Tomorrow couldn't come soon enough.

She was looking forward to having her friend in town.

****

The temperature hovered at one hundred degrees when Carrie left for the airport the next afternoon. After almost three weeks in the desert, she had grown accustomed to the heat, but she wondered how Phyllis would react to it.

"Oh my God, are we in Hell or what?" Phyllis exclaimed in her brash New York accent as they stepped through the automatic doors of the airport and into the hot Las Vegas sun.

Phyllis hugged her again as the driver loaded her bags into the trunk of the limousine. "Look at you. With that suntan. This city suits you well. You look gorgeous."

Carrie laughed and thanked her, but she hardly thought Las Vegas had done anything but turn her life upside down. Standing in the airport waiting for Phyllis's flight to land, she had wanted nothing more than to run to the nearest counter and buy a ticket for the next flight to New York. She didn't know how she'd make it through the next few days.

"So how's our client?" Phyllis asked when they were settled together in the backseat of the Grand Portofino's limousine. Her red hair was stuck to her forehead in the heat, and she leaned into the air-conditioning vent in an attempt to cool off.

"I have no idea," Carrie said, keeping her voice cheerful. "Though I'm sure he's very excited about the press event on Saturday."

"Don't play dumb with me." Phyllis patted her hand in a motherly fashion. "You know what I'm talking about."

"There's nothing to say. Things with Jack are finished."

"I'm sorry." Phyllis sighed. "I had high hopes for the two of you."

"Oh, Phyllis, you never give up."

"I'm not talking about your personal life. Though I'm truly sorry you're unhappy. You see," Phyllis said, adjusting the purse strap in her lap, "I was hoping you'd want to stay here and run Cresswell & Dailey West."

"What?" Carrie's eyes widened. She stared at her boss across the backseat of the limo.

"I was planning to talk to you about it later, but I guess now is as good a time as any." Phyllis turned toward Carrie. "With Vegas booming the way it is and so much business coming from the Grand Portofino, I thought this might be a good time to open an office here in Las Vegas."

Carrie couldn't believe her ears. She was glad she hadn't told Phyllis about Jack's job offer.

"I'm planning to feel things out while I'm here," Phyllis said. "Don't get your hopes up yet. It's just an idea."

A few days ago, the notion of relocating to Las Vegas to run a second office for Cresswell & Dailey would have been the perfect solution to all their problems. But after what had happened yesterday at the pool, the best thing to do was leave town, lick her wounds, and put the whole thing behind her. Living in the same city as Jack could prove nothing short of disastrous.

Except for Phyllis's occasional animated commentary as she looked out the window, they rode the rest of the way to the hotel in silence. When they arrived, Phyllis checked into her room, and they parted with plans to meet downstairs at Cardini's in an hour.

With Phyllis in town for the duration of her stay in Las Vegas, Carrie hoped she'd be able to keep Jack off her mind. But while meeting with Antonio and his crew in the restaurant, he sauntered in to say hello to Phyllis. Carrie cursed under her breath and avoided his gaze. She kept her eyes cast downward and pretended to read her notes.

"How nice to meet you." Jack shook Phyllis's hand as she stood from the table where they were holding their meeting. "I've heard so many wonderful things about you."

"I've heard wonderful things about *you*, too." Phyllis cast a knowing glance in Carrie's direction.

Carrie wanted to crawl under the table and die. She did not rise from her seat, nor did she dare look at Jack. His eyes, too, remained conspicuously diverted from her direction. If anyone else had picked up on the tension-drenched moment, they refrained from showing it.

It was the longest two minutes of her life. When he left the room, Carrie felt as if she'd had the wind knocked out of her. But she plastered on her best PR smile and kept working.

That evening, Sherry, Phyllis, and Carrie arranged to have dinner in Mark's suite at the hotel. Carrie thought it was important for her boss to meet all the key players on the Grand Portofino's leadership team, and Mark was more than eager for the company.

"So how are you feeling?" Sherry asked after introducing Phyllis to Mark. She set an oversized arrangement of fresh flowers on the desk.

"Better every day," Mark said. He was wearing a pair of cargo shorts and a UNLV tee shirt. "Please excuse me for not dressing up." This he directed at Phyllis, with a big smile.

Phyllis laughed, smiling as brightly as Carrie had ever seen. "Sherry told me about your little health scare. I hope you're feeling better," she said and literally batted her eyelashes.

"I am. Much better."

"How wonderful."

As if watching a tennis match, Carrie returned her

gaze to Mark to await his response. "Fifty-four years of healthy living, and I get taken down by a plate of spicy Cajun food." He laughed. "And I thought I was having a heart attack."

"I would hate to think of anything bad happening to your heart." Phyllis flashed him another smile.

Sherry and Carrie exchanged curious gazes, and Carrie had to bite her lip to stifle a giggle. It felt good to want to laugh again. Phyllis and Mark just sat there, staring at each other shamelessly.

At last, Sherry said, "I think we'd better order room service if we're going to call this a dinner meeting."

They ordered an array of seafood and pasta dishes and had dinner at the table in Mark's suite. Sherry was the first to rise when they were done. "It's getting late. We should let you get some rest, Mark."

"Yes." Carrie glanced at her phone. It was not quite eight o'clock, but she stood anyway and followed Sherry's lead. "We have a busy couple of days ahead."

"It's only eight," Phyllis interjected, clearly not having it. "I was just about to order a pot of coffee."

"There's a coffee maker over there," Mark said, pointing to the suite's kitchenette. "I'd love a cup, too, if you don't mind brewing it."

"Happy to." Phyllis popped up and went over to the counter. A moment later she turned back toward them with an exaggerated frown, waving a coffee mug in each of her hands. "Only two cups, though."

Carrie smirked. "I'm more of a morning coffee person, anyway."

Sherry glanced her way. "We could go get a real drink downstairs."

"What a great idea," Phyllis exclaimed before Carrie had a chance to respond. "You girls go to the casino to get yourselves a cocktail, and I'll make coffee here for me and Mark."

"Works for me," Mark said.

A few more awkward exchanges and Carrie and Sherry said goodnight, leaving Phyllis and Mark alone in his suite to drink coffee and whatever the heck else. Carrie had never seen her boss so flirtatious with a man, and it amused her to no end.

The hotel was just starting to get busy when they slipped into a lounge off the Grand Portofino's main casino floor.

"So what do you think that was all about?" Sherry asked when they were tucked side by side on two chairs at a high table near the bar. A band was setting up on the small circular stage near where they were sitting. "Is your boss single?"

"I *thought* she was married to her job," Carrie said. A cocktail waitress came to take their order. When she walked away, Carrie asked, "What about Mark? He seems like the type who always puts work before his personal life, too."

"I think he's lonely," Sherry mused, and Carrie nodded in thoughtful agreement. "He's been in Las Vegas for a very long time. My guess is he could use a woman in his life."

"Well, he shouldn't set his sights on Phyllis. She's leaving town on Sunday."

"A lot of things can happen between now and Sunday."

Carrie laughed. "Like what?"

"Vegas is a funny town," Sherry said. The waitress

arrived with their drinks and set them on the table. Sherry waited for her to leave before adding, over a sip of her Merlot, "Why do you think it's the marriage capital of the world? Something about this place makes people do crazy things. Even fall in love."

"I don't believe that." Carrie grimaced. God, this mess with Jack was turning her into a terrible cynic, and it was a side of herself she did not enjoy getting to know. She raised her margarita and took a long swallow.

"What about you and Jack?" Sherry challenged.

She nearly choked on her drink. "What about us?"

"Oh, come on. I'm not blind, Carrie."

Her breath caught in her throat. Did Sherry just say what she think she said? Carrie exhaled and then took another sip of her drink. "Is it that obvious?"

"Are you kidding?" Sherry laughed, unabashed. "The two of you might as well put an ad in *Las Vegas Sun*. Everybody knows."

"You're kidding." Carrie groaned. A wave of nausea washed over her.

"Come on, Carrie. We've known since the night you two got stuck in the elevator. Jack hasn't been the same man since you arrived in town." Sherry leaned conspiratorially over the table and lowered her voice a notch. "And did you really think I didn't know what was going on that night I found the two of you together in the hot tub at the villa? *Please*."

Carrie stared at her drink. She couldn't believe what Sherry was telling her. All those nights sneaking around, hiding in her suite, obsessing about getting caught...and they had all known anyway?

"Well," Carrie stammered, "what did people

think?"

"We thought Jack never looked happier. And believe me, when you've known him as long as I have, it's nice to see the man excited about something other than work."

Hating herself for sounding so meek, Carrie asked, "What did they think about me?"

"They all love you, Carrie." Seeing the concerned expression on Carrie's face, Sherry added, "What did you think we thought?"

That I was the office slut. That I traded blow jobs for this account. "I don't know."

"You can't control who you fall in love with," Sherry said. "I mean, we're all adults around here. We get our jobs done. Who cares who's sleeping with whom?"

Her face grew hot as sheer embarrassment engulfed her. She was glad they were sitting in a dark lounge.

"Jack's a great guy. I've worked in this town for a long time, and I can honestly say I've never met a more genuine person. Believe me," Sherry said, her voice emphatic. "Most men in Las Vegas are after one thing. And you know I'm not talking about good conversation. But not Jack. That man's got class."

"Well," Carrie said, stirring her margarita absently. She looked Sherry straight in the eye. "Things are over between us. But I appreciate your understanding."

"Too bad. Because it was starting to look to me like Jack might finally settle down."

Carrie shook her head, mulling over Sherry's words. The irony of learning all this now was nothing short of cruel.

The band launched into their set, filling the room

with upbeat pop classics. She was grateful for the interruption. With the lounge act performing, she didn't feel pressure to continue their conversation. The loud music made it impossible to talk without having to shout, and though the band was far from her usual taste in music, she was grateful to have a few minutes to think about what Sherry had said.

She finished her margarita. The waitress came around to check on them, and she was relieved when Sherry, too, declined the offer for a second drink. After a little while, Sherry signed the tab to her hotel expense account and said she was heading home for the night. Carrie stayed in the lounge until the band finished their set, thinking about Jack and what Sherry had told her, then went upstairs to her suite.

She called Phyllis, but there was no answer. Puzzled, Carrie set down her phone. Phyllis couldn't still be in Mark's suite, could she? It was after ten o'clock.

She crawled into bed, but her mind was racing too hard to even think about sleep. It was Thursday night, and the press party was only two days away, but Carrie was beginning to wonder if she could make it. Any more incidents with Jack, like the one in the restaurant earlier today, and she was afraid her heart might split in two. And after what Sherry had said tonight about everyone knowing, she didn't think she'd be able to even look her other colleagues in the eye without dying of embarrassment.

Maybe Jack's idea wasn't such a bad one, after all. With Phyllis now in town, Carrie could easily return to New York. It wasn't what she wanted to do, but it was starting to sound like the wisest choice. Everything was set for Saturday. Without a doubt, Phyllis and Megan could handle the event's execution.

She rolled over onto her side. She realized it might look like she was running away, but that wasn't the case at all. Wouldn't it be better to leave now, before things between her and Jack turned even uglier?

Tomorrow was Friday. If she caught an afternoon flight, she'd be back in New York in time for the weekend. Then she could really start to move on with her life.

Feeling a weight lift as she made the decision, Carrie drifted off to sleep. By this time tomorrow, she would be in her own bed in New York City, and Las Vegas, Jack Dillon, and everything that had happened in the last three weeks would be a distant memory.

****

The ringing of her phone woke Carrie up. She groped for it and answered it with a gruff, "Hello?"

"Good morning." Phyllis's cheery voice greeted her.

She sat up in bed. "What time is it?"

"Seven-fifteen," Phyllis said. "Oh sorry, I forget my body is still on New York time. Damn jet lag. Did you sleep well?"

"Where were you so late last night?" Carrie pushed her disheveled hair out of her face and rubbed her eyes. "I tried calling, but there was no answer on your cell or in your room."

"I spent the night in Mark's suite." Before Carrie could admonish her, Phyllis added, "On the couch. We were talking until late. I ended up just sleeping there."

"Phyllis, your suite is right down the hall from his."

"I fell asleep," Phyllis said, her defensive tone a thin veil. "So what's going on?"

Carrie took a deep breath. "I've decided to go back to New York. Today."

A moment of silence, and then, "Oh dear. You're serious."

"Yes."

"Okay." Phyllis sighed. "Meet me in the coffee shop in ten minutes. We should talk about this in person."

Carrie changed into a pair of jeans and a fresh white Oxford shirt. She washed her face and headed to the elevator. Her stomach was in knots. The two women were friends, but Carrie had to remember before anything else, Phyllis was also her boss. She hoped her decision to leave Las Vegas would not be an issue.

Phyllis was already in the coffee shop when Carrie arrived. She slid into the booth across from her and smiled, feeling anxious and more than a little out of her element. Carrie prided herself on always being more of a lean-in kind of girl, not someone who would ever choose to step back.

"Spill," Phyllis said after a minute had passed. "Because I know you can't be so sick of this tropical paradise, you can't wait another day to get back to that hot, dirty city."

Carrie took a deep breath and began to tell her the whole story, including her conversation with Sherry. The waitress came by to take their order, and by the time Carrie finished recapping, she was nibbling on buttered toast. She waited for Phyllis's reaction.

"Well," Phyllis said and took a thoughtful sip from

her second cup of coffee. "If flying home to New York today is what you feel you need to do, I won't stop you. I think you should be at the event since it was your brainchild, but Megan will be here later today, and she and I can certainly handle it. Just make sure you give me all your notes and the guest list before you go. And don't you dare breathe a word to Jim Cresswell about any of this."

Carrie nodded, feeling forlorn and more than a little guilty. She hated the idea of handing this event over to Phyllis and a junior account executive. But at the moment, it seemed like the lesser of two evils.

They finished their breakfast and promised to meet later to go over her notes for the party. She went back to her suite to shower, pack, and hop online to book the five o'clock flight to New York.

With nothing else to do until her one o'clock meeting with Phyllis, she sat at her desk by the window and surveyed the Strip below. The sun was hot on her face and sparkled off the buildings lining Las Vegas Boulevard. She found it hard to believe that in less than three weeks, she had grown so attached to this city. Leaving Las Vegas to go to New York felt more like she was leaving home than returning to it.

Taking a solemn look around her suite and the pile of luggage waiting by the door, she sighed again. The possibility of running into Jack distressed her, but she'd better go tell Sherry the news before Phyllis beat her to it.

****

Carrie found Sherry in the kitchen of Cardini's, talking to Antonio and sampling the dishes he was preparing for the party tomorrow night. The kitchen was the busiest she'd ever seen it, filled with chefs and busboys buzzing about, and smelled of Italian spices and bread baking in the ovens. Her stomach growled as she took in the wonderful scents.

"Got a second?" Carrie asked. She declined Antonio's offer for a taste of his bruschetta.

"Sure." Sherry put her fork on the counter and followed her to the rear of the kitchen, the expression on her face seized by concern.

"I'm headed back to New York," she said when they were out of earshot of Antonio and his staff. "Tonight."

"Oh, no. Is everything okay?"

"Yes." Carrie sighed. She didn't want to sound unprofessional, but she owed it to Sherry to be honest. And she trusted Sherry would understand, especially after their talk last night. "I just think leaving is the best thing to do."

Sherry offered her a sympathetic smile. "Carrie, I hope you don't mind me saying this, but have you thought this through? You said yourself you were worried we'd find out about your relationship with Jack. But we all knew, and nobody has a problem with it. So why are you leaving? Why not talk to him and see if you can work it out."

Carrie offered her a grateful smile. "I wish it were so simple, Sherry. But it's not just about people finding out. It's about Jack wanting to be in control and not let me make my own decisions. I almost married a guy like that once before, and I was miserable. I refuse to let myself end up in the same kind of relationship again."

Sherry nodded in understanding. "Phyllis told me she is flying out another staff member to help with the party tomorrow night. I'm sure between the two of them it will be fine, but I wish you were going to be here, too. This event has been your baby from the get-go. Are you sure you can't stay?"

Carrie shook her head. "I don't think so." She appreciated Sherry's support and would miss working with her. The two had so much in common and got along so well, she was certain they would have molded a close friendship had things with Jack gone the other way, and she decided to stay in Las Vegas.

"I hope everything works out for you, Carrie." Sherry gave her an impulsive hug. "I'm sure we'll talk soon."

"Will you tell Jack goodbye?"

"Sure," Sherry agreed.

"But wait until tomorrow morning, after I'm gone."

Sherry smoothed her dark hair with her hand. She did not look pleased by the request, but she nodded in agreement. "What time is your flight?"

"Five."

"Do you need a ride to the airport? I can arrange for the limo. Or give you a ride."

"No, I'll take a taxi." She forced a grateful smile. "I think it's better if I just slip away without a fuss."

Exiting the restaurant, Carrie floundered in a daze of sadness. She paused in the doorway, taking a final look around. Cardini's was decorated and set for the press event tomorrow night, the party she had envisioned and worked so tirelessly to bring to fruition. It was hard to believe she wouldn't be here to witness its success.

Chapter Sixteen

Ever since he saw Carrie at Cardini's the day Phyllis arrived, Jack had been overwrought with guilt. These past two days without her had left him miserable, unable to sleep or concentrate. He couldn't believe their relationship had plummeted to the point where they couldn't even make eye contact.

It was his fault, he realized. He had told her to leave. He thought not having to see her would clear his mind to focus on work, but it turned out the opposite was true. He couldn't stop thinking about her at all or the ocean of regret drowning him at every turn.

Jack hadn't meant for the conversation to go so awry when he saw her by the pool the other day. He wanted to talk to her and knowing Carrie had fallen into the habit of lounging by the pool each afternoon, it seemed like a good opportunity to catch her alone. What he wasn't prepared for though was the sight of her emerging from the pool, beads of water sparkling off her perfect body, and the white bathing suit clinging to her every curve, just the tiniest bit see-through. He couldn't help but remember what those curves looked like with her bathing suit off.

And as he stood watching her, hating himself for hovering in the shadow of the cabana rental booth like a psycho stalker, he got angry. He thought of all the women in his past, the ones who had used him. The ones he had ended things with before he got in too deep. And here was Carrie, sitting on a lounge chair with her wet, golden skin shimmering in the sun; a woman who had never asked him for a thing but still ended up pummeling him. It was too much for his stupid pride to handle, so he'd ordered her to go home.

But she didn't. The woman had said no to his face, and that pissed him off. And turned him on. Because everything Carrie did turned him on. And then that pissed him off even more.

Jack didn't need her to explain the importance of putting her career first. He had been doing the same thing all his life. It would be hypocritical of him not to respect her for it and do whatever he could to support her dreams. He wished he had told her that instead.

The bottom line was, he missed her. They belonged together. The realization hit him with the force of a freight train.

He couldn't change the past, but he could control the future. It was something he'd learned after more than a decade of building hotels. And whatever it took to make Carrie understand he was playing for keeps, Jack was prepared to do it.

So now, on this sunny Saturday morning, he drove to the Grand Portofino with the radio playing loud and a smile on his face. The wind danced through the open sunroof and ruffled his hair. He pushed it back with one hand while tapping along to the radio with his other. The song was a classic rock favorite, fast and upbeat, with a killer guitar riff. It matched his optimistic mood, and he turned up the volume.

The moment he arrived in his office, he called Carrie's suite.

"Pick up, dammit," he said, growing impatient as he listened to the incessant ring on the other end of the receiver. When there was no answer on her room phone, he called her cell. Then he called Phyllis, but her phone also went unanswered.

"Where the hell are my PR people?" Jack shouted in frustration to nobody in particular. He was alone in his office on the thirtieth floor.

He stood from his desk, determined not to get discouraged, but feeling his optimistic mood slip away. He ran his hand through his hair and thought for a moment. She must be at Cardini's getting ready for the grand opening, too busy to hear her phone ring.

He took the elevator to the lobby and crossed the crowded casino floor, heading toward the restaurant. Cardini's was abuzz with workers getting ready for the party, but when he scanned the room, neither Carrie nor Phyllis Dailey were in sight.

Chaos consumed the kitchen as Jack crossed through it. The clamor of pots banging and chefs calling to each other filled the room as Antonio and his team prepared for the event. He spotted Frank leaning against a stainless steel counter, pouring over a pile of paperwork.

"Have you seen Carrie Thomas?" Jack asked, forcing his voice to sound casual.

"Oh, she's gone," Frank said, not looking up from the stack of invoices he was combing through.

Jack froze in his tracks. "What do you mean, gone?"

"She went back to New York." Frank glanced at Jack. "I thought you knew. I heard her telling Sherry yesterday."

"Nobody told me." Jack masked his bruised ego behind an angry façade, his features strained and tight. He knew Carrie was upset, but he couldn't believe she would leave town without saying goodbye. Moreover, he couldn't believe she left town at all after her big speech about seeing her project through.

"You okay?" Frank asked, brow furrowing as he noticed the dark expression that had crept over Jack's face.

"Yeah, just surprised." Jack crossed his arms in annoyance. "I mean, who's going to run the press event?"

"Phyllis, I guess." Frank continued shuffling through the invoices on the counter. "From what I gather, she's got it covered. Been working on it with Carrie from New York for the last three weeks."

Jack dug his hands into the pockets of his dark suit pants. The news of Carrie's departure hit him like a brutal punch in the stomach.

"Are you sure you're okay?" Frank asked again. "You look like shit."

"Yeah, I'm fine," Jack said, brushing off Frank's blunt show of concern. "Listen, I'll be in my office if you need anything. Otherwise, I'll see you at the party tonight."

He left the restaurant before Frank asked any more questions. He had to find Sherry and figure out exactly what Carrie had said about going back to New York, and why the hell nobody had let him know their PR person was leaving town.

Since it was the weekend, the resort's executive offices were near empty as Jack strode through the department. He found Sherry at her desk. Except for the sunlight pouring in through the window of her office and spilling into the hall through her open door, the rest of the area was dark and quiet.

Without saying a word, he stood in her open doorway until she noticed him there and looked up from her computer. "Oh, hey, Jack."

"When were you planning to tell me Carrie Thomas was gone?" Jack asked, a thick layer of annoyance shadowing his voice.

Sherry's face fell. "So she decided to tell you herself, after all."

"No." He stepped inside her office. "Frank told me."

"Frank?" Her voice rose in surprise. She stood from her chair behind the desk. "He must have heard the two of us talking in the kitchen yesterday."

"Great," Jack said, his voice weighted with an uncharacteristic shot of sarcasm. "So everybody knows she left for New York except me."

"Carrie asked me not to tell you until today," Sherry said. "I went upstairs and looked for you when I got here first thing this morning, but you weren't in yet."

He sighed. There was no point lashing out at Sherry for a situation he had brought on himself. "Well, what did she tell you?"

Sherry took a deep breath, looking profoundly uncomfortable with whatever she was about to say. "She wanted to return to New York to—"

"You know what?" Jack interrupted, raising a hand to silence her. He didn't want to drag Sherry into this any more than she already was, and he really didn't want to know what Carrie had told her. "It doesn't matter. I'm sure Phyllis will do a fine job managing the press event. I just want the whole damn thing to be over."

"But Jack, if you'll just listen for a minute…" She circled her desk and followed him.

He knew he was being a jerk, first sweeping into her office and demanding answers, then leaving before she could even give them to him. He'd apologize later. Right now, he just wanted to be left the hell alone. He kept walking down the dark, empty corridor and did not turn around.

That didn't stop Sherry from calling after him as he retreated. "She's still in love with you, too!"

Chapter Seventeen

Carrie took a taxi to the airport Friday afternoon like she planned and even made it through the security checkpoint and to her gate. But sitting in the terminal waiting for her flight to board—watching excited tourists arrive, departing tourists take one last crack at the airport slot machines, and executive-types dart by with rolling suitcases in tow—she had the acute realization her time in Vegas was not done.

She was no quitter, and damn Jack Dillon before his icy treatment sent her running back to New York City. This was her event, and Hell would have to freeze over before she missed it.

Carrie collected her luggage and grabbed another taxi straight back to the hotel. She checked into the Grand Portofino, using her own credit card and opting for a standard room instead of the suite Jack had furnished her with during the time she'd been working there.

As soon as she was settled, she picked up her phone and called Phyllis's cell, but once again her boss wasn't answering. Mark's phone, too, went unanswered. She wondered what the two of them were up to, especially since Mark was still under doctor's orders to take it easy.

At last, she gave up and went to bed. She'd have plenty of time to explain things to Phyllis tomorrow.

It was almost ten o'clock on Saturday morning by the time Carrie was dressed and ready to face the day. Another call to Phyllis proved fruitless, so she left the hotel and caught a cab to the Forum Shops at Caesars Palace on the other end of the Strip. Unless she wanted to wear the same blue dress for the third time in two weeks, she needed to buy something new for the press event tonight.

It took her the better part of the day to find the perfect dress, a pale ivory designer gown that exceeded her budget but seemed worthy of the price tag. Tonight was a pivotal point in her career; Carrie wanted to look and feel her best and knew in this dress she would. Plus, retail therapy always improved her mood. She returned to the hotel, confident and excited about the night ahead.

On impulse, she stopped by Phyllis's suite on the way to her room. She was surprised when the door opened.

"Carrie." Phyllis threw her arms around the younger woman's shoulders. "What are you doing here?" She pulled her into the room and shut the door.

Setting her garment bag over the back of a chair, Carrie said, "I changed my mind. This is my event, and I want to be here for it."

Phyllis smiled but looked skeptical. "Are you sure you're up for it? I've got Megan there now supervising the final setup."

"Absolutely." She flashed Phyllis a bright, confident smile, not wanting her boss to doubt her capabilities for even a second. "I've got this."

"And what about Jack?"

"Tonight, he's just a client." Carrie's voice was far

more self-assured than she felt.

She didn't tell Phyllis the last thing she wanted was for Jack to think she'd fled to New York because she couldn't handle seeing him. No, she wanted her last encounter with Jack to be one where she stood tall and in control, kicking ass and taking names. Blowing this press event out of the water. That's how she wanted Jack to remember her. She would say a proper goodbye and give their affair closure. Even if her heart was shattering into a million pieces on the inside, on the outside, she was determined to be all polish and professionalism.

"So where were you all day?" Carrie looked around the room. Except for the cell phone charging on the nightstand and an unpacked suitcase with its top flipped open on the bed, it looked like Phyllis had spent almost no time in the room at all. "I've been trying to get a hold of you since last night."

"Mark and I decided to take a drive into the desert," Phyllis said, smiling dreamily. "We took a hike in Red Rock Canyon. I've never been to this part of the country before. It's quite beautiful."

"I think so, too," Carrie agreed, remembering the time she and Jack drove through the desert and made love under the stars. That night may as well have been a million years ago.

"We stopped at an old silver mining town for lunch," Phyllis continued, more to herself than to Carrie. "It was a wonderful day."

Carrie smiled, glad to see her friend so happy. She gathered her purse and the garment bag. "Well, I'd better go get ready. I'll call Sherry from my room and let her know I'll be there for the event, after all."

"Good idea," Phyllis said. "I'll meet you in your room, and we can go downstairs together."

"Sounds good. I'll text you my new room number."

Phyllis walked her to the door. "And, Carrie, I'm glad you decided to stay. I know it was a difficult decision, and I'm proud you made the right one."

Carrie smiled. She was glad she had made the right decision, too.

****

Carrie rushed to her hotel room, realizing she had less than an hour to get ready before the first guests arrived. She wanted to be at Cardini's early and make sure everything was perfect. She took a quick shower, then styled her hair into a soft upsweep. Standing in front of the mirror, she couldn't decide if she was more anxious about the event itself or the fact she would be seeing Jack for the last time before returning to New York in the morning.

Phyllis arrived while she was still in her robe, putting on the last touches of her makeup.

"Are you almost ready to go?" Phyllis followed her into the bathroom. She was wearing a conservative black dress and coordinating jacket.

"In a minute." Carrie resumed applying her mascara. "I want to make sure I look good in case I end up in any photos." The lie tasted ridiculous on her tongue. She was sure even Phyllis knew the real reason for her meticulous attention to her appearance.

Carrie dabbed on a fresh coat of lip gloss. "So Sherry told me Mark was feeling well enough to go to the party tonight."

"Yes." Phyllis met her gaze in the mirror. She had that dreamy smile on her face again.

"Okay, I have to ask." Carrie turned to face her. She had never seen her boss act like such a schoolgirl in love. "Is there something going on between the two of you?"

Phyllis shrugged. "We'll see. He's a very nice man." But Carrie could tell there was a lot more to it. Her eyes narrowed as Phyllis exited the bathroom.

Carrie followed her out, then crossed to the closet and removed her dress from the protective plastic garment bag. She shed her robe to reveal a set of lacy lingerie, then pulled the ivory dress over her head.

"Zip me up, please." She turned her back to Phyllis, who proceeded to secure Carrie into the dress.

"I see we've gone for the conservative business approach," Phyllis said, a sarcastic twinge in her voice. Her gaze swept over the floor-length ivory gown. But she also told her the dress was beautiful. "I'd steer clear of the red wine, though," she added. The pale dress bordered on white, and while it flattered Carrie's slim figure and golden tan, the color was also unforgiving.

Carrie grabbed her beaded handbag and leather portfolio with all her notes for the event. "Ready?"

Cardini's was already buzzing with people when the two women arrived. Cocktail waitresses dressed in short red dresses offered drinks and hors d'oeuvres to the guests. A trio of musicians played in the corner.

"Hey, you made it!" Carrie turned to find her colleague coming toward them. Young and pretty, with shoulder-length dark blonde hair and a splatter of freckles over the bridge of her nose, Megan Summers looked genuinely happy to see her. "The gang's all here."

"Thanks for taking charge this afternoon." Carrie

gave her a quick, warm hug. "The place looks fantastic."

"Thank you," Megan said, a proud smile on her face. "It's been fun, and I'm happy to help." She wandered off to check on a few final details.

Sherry approached and introduced Carrie and Phyllis to Jack's business associates who had flown in from San Francisco for the event. Antonio Cardini had arrived as well, the picture of European suaveness in his tuxedo.

"Are you ready for your speech?" Carrie asked, brushing a stray piece of lint from his jacket. It was second nature to make sure the star of her show was camera-ready. "This room will be packed with reporters very soon."

Phyllis and Carrie chatted with Antonio for a few minutes, reviewing last-minute details and making final edits to his speaking points.

"Oh, there's Mark." Phyllis spotted him across the room and darted over to say hello. Carrie watched her boss kiss him on the cheek before the two engaged in an animated conversation. Watching them laughing across the room reminded her of Jack, and she scanned the restaurant for him. But he was nowhere to be seen. Her heart dipped. After all their planning, Jack wouldn't have decided to skip the press event, would he?

"Excuse me, are you Carrie Thomas?"

Carrie turned her attention to the man standing beside her and smiled her most professional smile. "Yes. Hello."

He shook her hand. "Brett Bender, Dallas Morning News. We talked on the phone last week about the review I'm writing for the travel section. I wanted to ask you a couple of questions."

Carrie spent the next hour circulating the room, immersed in conversation with various reporters. She was pleased so many of the journalists who had committed to attending the event were there. It was always a publicist's worst nightmare to throw a press party without any press. But tonight, they had definitely shown up. She beamed with pride, relieved the event was packing a full house.

Amid the buzz, the night was racing by. Carrie was so entrenched in talking to guests and making sure things were running on schedule, Jack had remarkably slipped her mind. But then she spotted him on the other side of the restaurant, and her heart screeched to a halt.

Never in her entire life had she seen a man look so handsome. Dressed in a traditional black and white tuxedo, with his hair slicked back, Jack looked more like he had stepped out of the pages of a men's fashion magazine than the owner of the hotel.

He looked up and caught her staring from across the room, and his face lit up. The two stood frozen, a sea of people separating them. Carrie felt her heart soften, all the animosity dissolving like a summer breeze blowing dew off a bed of flowers in the morning. She couldn't even remember what their fight had been about.

He began walking toward her, but Frank Giotto stepped into his path and interrupted to introduce him to someone. She watched the three men chatting until her own attention was diverted by a reporter who approached to say hello. Talking to Jack would have to wait a little while longer.

Carrie and Antonio were speaking to Amy Muller, an Entertainment Editor for the *Las Vegas Valley Sentinel*, when she saw him again. He stood with Phyllis not ten feet away, heads leaned close, and it was obvious whatever they were talking about was private and very important. Under normal circumstances, she would never eavesdrop on one of Phyllis's conversations, but tonight the stakes were high. She strained to listen, but the live music and chatter of guests filling the room made it impossible for her to decipher their words.

"So what specialties are you including on the menu here that are exclusive to the Grand Portofino?" Amy asked, recapturing Carrie's attention. She adjusted her retro '90s butterfly-shaped barrette to capture a long lock of wavy brown hair that kept falling in front of her eyes.

Carrie gestured for Antonio to answer the question. He launched into an animated description of his famous Tomato and Olive-Marinated Bocconcini, and she allowed her attention to wander back to Jack and Phyllis.

This time when Jack caught her eye, he did not look away. She held his gaze with questioning eyes. Phyllis turned to see what had stolen Jack's attention, and when she saw Carrie, excitedly motioned for her to come over.

"Excuse me," she said, leaving Antonio alone with the reporter. She waded through the crowd, bracing for the encounter.

Just then, Sherry's voice boomed through the loudspeakers, capturing the attention of the room. She welcomed everyone to the Grand Portofino and announced dinner was about to be served. As everyone moved to find their seats, Jack flashed Carrie an apologetic smile. "Later," his eyes told her. He turned and made his way to the front of the room.

She slid into her chair and took a sip of water. Phyllis took her seat between Carrie and Megan at their table. Carrie leaned her way and whispered, "What were you two talking about?"

"Shh." Phyllis joined in the applause as Sherry introduced Jack to the crowd. He strode to the podium with long, confident strides.

Carrie settled her gaze on him. Jack was a naturally exuberant speaker, commanding the room with his deep voice and good humor. Even though she had written most of the speech, she sat entranced, listening to him deliver it. He spoke with such pride, not only for the hotel he had built but of the people who helped run it. Her heart swelled. This was a big night for him, and she was glad Jack was having his moment in the spotlight.

As Jack turned his remarks to Cardini's and how pleased he was to have the new restaurant call the Grand Portofino home, Carrie heard two of the cocktail waitresses whispering behind her.

"Screw the Italian food; I'd like to eat him," one of them said. They both burst into giggles.

Carrie glared at the two young women, and appropriately scolded, they stopped laughing and scampered to the other side of the room. She smiled with satisfaction but had to remind herself tonight Jack was just her client, not the man she was still in love with. She had no right to be possessive. Nonetheless, her cheeks burned. She took a long drink from her water glass.

"So with no further ado," Jack announced from the podium, "I give you the very talented, Antonio Cardini!"

The room burst into applause. Antonio approached the front of the room, and the two men shook hands and posed for photos before Antonio began his speech. Carrie's gaze followed Jack as he returned to his seat on the other side of the restaurant.

Would they ever get the chance to say goodbye?

Chapter Eighteen

It was after ten when the event concluded. Stuffed with pancetta and pasta and a forbidden piece of cheesecake, Carrie made the rounds, saying goodnight to the journalists and VIPs who had attended. After weeks of planning and all her hard work, the press event was a huge success, and for that she was glad. But she was also thankful to have the night behind her.

Carrie couldn't wait to get a moment alone with Phyllis to ask what she and Jack had been talking about earlier, but she hadn't seen her since before dessert. It wasn't like Phyllis to act so flighty, especially during an important business function. The mystery of it all left Carrie both curious and on edge. She dabbed on a fresh coat of lip gloss and scanned the room for her boss.

Most of the guests had moved on to the private party being held in the hotel's nightclub, the Riviera Room. But with her early flight in the morning, Carrie chose to skip that part of the event. Megan was already there, and Carrie was confident her colleague could handle the scene on her own. She said goodbye to the last of the guests inside the restaurant.

"Thanks for coming." She shook Brett Bender's hand. "I hope your story turns out great."

"I'll make sure you get a copy," he said with a wink. "It'll be a good one." Brett looked eager to head to the nightclub. He had spent the entire time during dinner downing rum and Cokes while entertaining their table of eight with stories of his wild Texas escapades, and Carrie had not missed his obvious perusal of the Grand Portofino's cocktail waitresses. They were also moving on to the party in the Riviera Room.

"Have fun," Carrie called as Brett exited the restaurant. She was tempted to add a sarcastic "good luck," but with his rugged looks and suave Southern charm, she figured luck was the last thing a man like Brett Bender needed when it came to women.

"There you are." At the sound of her boss's voice, Carrie spun around to find Phyllis approaching with Mark in tow. They were holding hands.

"How are you feeling?" Carrie asked, giving Mark a quick hug. This was the first chance she had to talk to him all night.

"Best I've ever felt," he said, grinning at Phyllis. Phyllis beamed right back at him as she squeezed her body against Mark's arm.

"Okay, enough already." Carrie bit her lip to stifle a full-blown laugh. "What's going on with you two?"

Phyllis giggled. Carrie had never heard her boss giggle before, and it was strikingly out of character. She arched an eyebrow.

"We're getting married!" Phyllis gushed.

"What?" Carrie's mouth dropped open in surprise.

Mark raised their entwined hands to show Carrie the ring adorning Phyllis's finger. He must have just presented it to her because Carrie would have noticed if she'd been wearing that rock at dinner. It was a huge pear-shaped diamond, at least double the size of the ring David had given her when he proposed. Phyllis dropped Mark's hand so Carrie could get a closer look at the engagement ring.

"Wow, congratulations," she said, giving Phyllis a hug. She was thrilled the two of them had found each other but overwhelmed by the quickness of their decision.

"When? Where?" Carrie asked, shaking her head with disbelief.

"Oh, that's all yet to be decided."

"I'm hoping by Christmas," Mark said. Phyllis's face lit up, and the two exchanged a kiss.

"But you've only known each other two days." Carrie didn't mean to sound negative, but she couldn't believe her ears.

"What did I tell you?" Phyllis asked. "When you find true love, grab on and don't let go. I knew the minute I laid my eyes on this man, he was the one for me."

"That goes double for me," Mark said, and he and Phyllis kissed again.

Watching them paw each other, Carrie did her best to push away the unwelcome surge of envy. Without thinking, she scanned the room for Jack.

As if reading her mind, Mark said, "I think Jack went over to the Riviera Room."

"Oh." Carrie dropped her gaze to the floor as disappointment washed over her. Guess she wasn't going to get that closure with him, after all. But she didn't want to spoil the mood for Phyllis and Mark. She plastered on her best smile and asked, "Where will you two live? Back in New York?"

"No." Mark chuckled. "Too cold for my desert blood."

"Remember what I started to tell you the other

day?" Phyllis asked. "About opening a second office here in Las Vegas? Well, I'm doing it."

"What about Jim Cresswell?" Carrie asked. "What does he think of all this?"

"Didn't I tell you?" Phyllis shook her head. "Oh my, I guess with all the excitement around here, I plain forgot."

"Tell me what?"

Phyllis placed a hand on Carrie's arm. "Carrie, I bought him out. The old geezer's retiring to Miami Beach at the end of the month."

"Oh my goodness." Carrie was stunned by the news. Jim had been considering retirement, but she had no idea it would happen so soon. The whammies just kept coming. "I'm so excited for you."

"And for you too," Phyllis said. "I'm going to be bi-coastal and work out of both offices. Half my time in New York, and half my time here in Vegas with this amazing man." She gave Mark the most obnoxious, loving smile Carrie had ever seen. She wanted to be happy for them, but right now, it was a little too much for her heart and stomach to handle.

Phyllis turned to her with a serious expression. "My offer still stands. You're the best account executive I've got, and if you want to relocate to Las Vegas and run the new office—with a big promotion and raise included, of course—the job is yours."

"Oh, wow," Carrie said. She was flattered by her boss's offer but knew with the way things stood with Jack, there was no way she could move to this city. She'd wait for a more appropriate time to officially turn down the opportunity, though. When she could talk to Phyllis alone. "I'll have to think about it."

Only a handful of people remained in the restaurant. Around them, busboys were clearing dessert dishes off the tables, and two tech guys were disconnecting the sound system at the front of the room. She stepped aside as the trio of musicians went by with their packed-up instruments.

Mark checked his watch. "Well, we're headed over to the club," he said to Carrie. "Care to join us?"

"No, thanks." Carrie yawned for emphasis. The two men breaking down the sound system loaded the podium and speakers onto a cart. They wheeled them out of the room. "I think it's bedtime for me."

"Great job tonight." Phyllis hugged her again. "Oh, by the way, I changed my flight to the redeye tomorrow night, so I'll see you in the office on Monday."

This news saddened her even further. Perhaps it was selfish, but she was looking forward to the four-hour flight home in the morning with Phyllis to lament over Jack. Now she would have to fly home by herself.

Alone in the restaurant, Carrie sank into a chair at one of the deserted tables and rested her face in the palms of her hands.

This was not how she had imagined this night to end. What should have been the happiest night in her professional life had instead left her feeling utterly depressed. A hot rush of tears sprang to her eyes and, shaking, she smothered a sob in her throat.

"Don't cry," a familiar voice implored from behind.

Carrie turned to find Jack standing there. In his formal tuxedo, he looked even more incredible up close. Like James Bond, except younger and with a nicer ass. His face was clean-shaven, and as much as she loved him with a five o'clock shadow, tonight the clear-cut lines of his profile were exquisite. She thought of the two cocktail waitresses who had been ogling him during his speech. *I'd like to eat him, too.*

She wiped the tears away from her eyes in one swift motion. "I thought you went over to the Riviera Room."

Jack pulled out a chair and sat beside her. "I came back to find you."

"Oh." Carrie nodded and blinked away the tears still clouding her eyes. God, she was tired of crying all the time. She looked around the near-empty restaurant, willing herself to get it together and hoping her face was not all red and splotchy. So much for polished and professional.

"You did an amazing job here tonight," Jack said. "You should be very proud."

"Thank you."

A palpable tension lingered between them, and they sat in silence for a few long moments. One of the busboys came by and started clearing off the table where they were sitting. Jack gave him a kind but commanding smile. "Would you gentlemen mind excusing us, please?"

The busboy nodded and glanced over to his colleagues. All three exited to the kitchen and shut the door, leaving Carrie and Jack alone in the restaurant.

Jack fidgeted with the silverware on the table. "Sherry told me you left town yesterday," he said, his gaze fixed on the silverware he was touching. Carrie watched as he absently ran his thumb along the glinting silver handle of a dessert fork. "I was surprised when I saw you here tonight."

"I changed my mind," she said. "I didn't want to leave without saying goodbye. Besides"—she sat up straight in her chair—"this was my project, and I wanted to see it through to the end."

Jack managed a quirky smile, his expression a jumble of pride and sadness and infinite regret. "That's my girl," he said, and Carrie's heart broke a little more.

Jack started to reach for her but caught himself and dropped his hand to the table. "Are you still leaving in the morning?"

"Yes," she answered. "I'm already packed."

He absorbed this news with a stony expression. "Congratulations on your big promotion. I know it's what you wanted. Phyllis told me about the new office she's opening in Vegas. Will you be running it?"

She stared at her lap, then shook her head. "I don't think so, Jack. After everything that's happened between us, I think going back to New York would be the smartest thing to do. I'm sure whoever Phyllis hires to manage your account here in Las Vegas will do a fine job."

"It's not my account I care about."

Carrie bit the inside of her cheek, refusing to meet his gaze. How could he expect her to move to Las Vegas and pretend like nothing ever happened between them? Maybe Jack could go on with business as usual, but her heart was not that strong…no matter how big a promotion Phyllis offered her.

"I should get going," Carrie said. She had said her goodbyes, and there was nothing left to say.

But as she rose, he halted her escape with a firm hand on her forearm. "Wait."

Just one word. It caused her heart to skip a beat,

and her whole life flashed before her. Like she was teetering over the edge of a cliff and about to fall. Or fly. *Wait.*

"I'm sorry about what I said the other day." Jack swallowed the pride that had become his worst enemy. There was a pained expression on his face. "I need you to know, I never wanted you to leave. Seeing you here at the hotel every day was just...too hard. I couldn't stand having to face you, knowing you didn't want me."

Now Carrie looked at him, astonished by his admission. "I did want you," she stated. And then before she could stop herself, added, "I still want you."

"But you told me—"

"I said I didn't want to *work* for you." Her voice dropped, dripping with honesty as she said, "But I never not wanted you."

His gaze raked over her with a longing tenderness.

She swallowed. "I didn't realize some sacrifices were worth making for love."

He shook his head. "I should have been more supportive. I gave up on us too easily."

"No, I did."

"You were so afraid of people finding out about us."

"And it turns out they all knew, anyway." A hint of a smile played at Carrie's lips as she spoke the words.

"And nobody cared," he said. "In fact, I think they were all rooting for us."

"Isn't it ironic?" Her expression erupted into a joyous grin. "And now we won't have to hide anything from anybody."

Jack took her hands in his and rose from his chair,

pulling her up, too. "Are you saying…"

Before he could finish, she dove into his arms, pressing her lips against his. He responded with an intense passion, wrapping his strong arms around her body and pulling her against him. She felt his chest drop in relief.

"I couldn't stop thinking about you the whole time." The words tumbled from Carrie's mouth between kisses. "I thought you hated me."

"I thought you hated me."

Jack's laughter mixed with hers, and she pressed her forehead to his. He kissed her again, softly at first, but then taking her mouth with a savage intensity. Her body responded instinctively, heat shooting from her core. She groaned into his mouth, hungry for more.

"I need to have you right now." He spoke in a husky whisper. "I'm sorry, but I don't think I can wait another minute."

"God, yes." Carrie barely got the words out before his mouth crashed to hers, lips molding together and tongues circling. His arms tightened around her. The kiss was everything she'd been missing these last several days, filling the cold void in her heart with heat and need.

In one swoop, she was on the table. Flat on her back, knees parted, with Jack standing wedged between her dangling legs. He pushed the fabric of her floor-length dress up her leg, grabbing the curve under one knee so he could lift her leg high, sending a stiletto clattering to the floor.

He kissed the top of her bare foot, and then seared a path from her ankle to her thigh, pushing the skirt of her ivory dress down as he went. The soft fabric shimmied against her leg. When his lips reached the top of her thigh, she arched her back.

"So beautiful," he murmured, pressing his mouth to the panel of her lacy panties. "God, I've missed this."

Carrie gasped at the exquisite feel of his touch. She grabbed a fistful of his hair, twisting it in her fingers as he teased her with his mouth. She pressed into him, unabashed.

Jack's hands swept over her thighs. He gripped the thin slice of lace on each side of her hips, tugging on the dainty lingerie while he worked her with his tongue through the fabric.

"I'm going to tear these off you," he stated, not asking for permission.

With one strong motion, he yanked the delicate fabric, and it came apart with a ferocious rip. She heard the clatter of silverware tumbling to the floor as his arms swept over the table and knocked it over the edge in his haste. The tattered remains of her lace panties fell to the table.

His mouth was now on her bare skin, licking and prodding at her opening, drawing from Carrie a guttural moan in a voice she didn't even recognize. She didn't care if they were still in the restaurant or that all the staff was just on the other side of the kitchen door. None of those things mattered.

She heard the delicious sound of his zipper opening. Not a slow, sensual inching down, but a fast, desperate *whoosh*. She craned her neck to see, releasing her grip on his hair. Jack held his cock in one hand and wiped his mouth using the back of his other. She licked her lips, hungry for him.

He reached into his pocket and pulled a condom

from his wallet, then tossed the wallet clumsily onto the table. "We'll be putting an end to using these things very soon," he mumbled. Carrie smiled at the permanence his promise evoked.

A moment later, he thrust inside her with a desperate force. She cried out and sat up, looping her arms around his neck as he drove into her again and again. Jack's strong arm came around her lower back, bracing her upright and close. Their mouths pressed together, and she groaned into him, feeling the heat rising through her body.

"Oh, God," Carrie cried, shattering in his arms. She dug her teeth into his shoulder. As she shuddered against him, Jack let out a visceral grunt and poured into her, breathing her name. He kissed the top of her head.

She laid back on the table, staring at the ceiling and breathing hard. Jack slid out of her and collapsed into a chair, wrapping the condom in one of the linen napkins discarded on the table.

Sitting up again, she laughed at their exuberance. She swung her legs off the table and hopped down, then sat on Jack's lap and kissed him.

He brushed the hair off her face. "That was amazing."

"Mmm." She rested her head on his shoulder, enjoying the calm, quiet afterglow and serenity of his nearness. She breathed him in, basking in his familiar scent and the feel of his heartbeat pulsing against her cheek.

"I never thought I'd hold you like this again." He stroked her hair tenderly. "And now, I'm never letting go. Please tell me you'll stay."

"I'll stay."

He kissed her again, this time long and deep and filled with the promise of forever. Her head spun in the wonder and ecstasy of the moment.

"I love you," Jack said, when, after what seemed like an eternity, he released her from their embrace.

Carrie's eyes glistened, but this time her tears were tears of happiness. It was amazing how fast life could take a turn. "I love you, too."

She released a deep, satisfied sigh. Everything was falling into place. She could keep her job with Cresswell & Dailey and still move to Las Vegas to be with Jack. She would be able to work with him without working *for* him. From here on out, they would face the world as a team.

"Marry me," Jack said suddenly. He looked at her with a determined intensity.

She answered without hesitation. "Yes."

"I mean tonight. Here at the hotel. Right now."

Carrie jumped off his lap, straightening her dress as she stood. The shock of his proposal was more than she expected, but she leaned into the moment. "I thought you said the wedding chapels were all booked solid."

"I own the hotel, Carrie." Jack laughed, standing up too and buckling his tuxedo pants. "I think we can work something out."

"But I don't even have a wedding dress."

"You're practically wearing white." He grabbed Carrie by the hand and twirled her around, then pulled her in tight. "I have never seen anyone look as beautiful as you do right now."

"Oh, Jack." She melted against him. She was never this spontaneous, but she had also never been more certain of anything in her entire life. It was time to let go of control and follow her heart. For once, she was confident it was leading her in the right direction.

"One more thing." The expression on Jack's face turned serious. He pulled away just enough to look into her eyes. "I heard what you said the other day about needing to be in control of your own life and career. And I understand and respect that. I know you can take care of yourself," he said. "I promise I'll never try to 'rescue' you again."

Carrie smiled at him in the coy way he loved, her finger hooked under the collar of his shirt. "Well," she confessed, pulling him back toward her, "maybe sometimes I need you to rescue me, after all."

A word about the author...

Author, travel writer, and PR professional, Gwen Kleist has been writing for as long as she can remember. In addition to writing romance, her work has been published in numerous publications, and she runs the travel website CaliforniaFamilyTravel.com.

Gwen lives with her husband and son in Southern California. When she's not writing or traveling, she loves spending time with friends and family.

Visit her at:

https://www.gwenkleist.com

Thank you for purchasing
this publication of The Wild Rose Press, Inc.

For questions or more information
contact us at
info@thewildrosepress.com.

The Wild Rose Press, Inc.
www.thewildrosepress.com

CPSIA information can be obtained
at www.ICGtesting.com
Printed in the USA
BVHW080019170921
616898BV00013B/662